ghostly

Paperback ISBN 978-1-989642-46-7
Ebook ISBN 978-1-989642-47-4
© 2024 Lintusen Press Shawn Bird, ed.

Lintusen Press
PO Box 10019
Salmon Arm BC
Canada V1E 3B9

ghostly

LINTUSEN
PRESS

FINNIAN BURNETT

The Ghosts Who Leave Us Behind

he ghosts moved into our house in July. *You want it to be a dark and stormy night*, Mary would say later, after it was all over, on those rare nights we would sit up late, lights burning and talk about what happened. *You want it to be scarier than it was*, she says sometimes, even still.

But it was hot and sunny, that July, and mid morning, not later than ten a.m., as we'd barely finished our coffee and Mary still had half a piece of toast on a small plate in front of her.

Jeffery was cramming frozen waffles into the toaster, eating them nearly as fast as they popped, drowning in syrup and butter. And I played with my coffee, as usual, and the remains of my scrambled eggs and wondered why it was so quiet, even though Jeffery jabbered on and on about something; I don't remember what. But it was silent, like we'd fallen into a vacuum, and I remember staring across the counter at Jeffery—his mouth moved and his eyes widened but no sound moved on the air between the two of us. And the ghosts moved in, stealthy and quiet at first. Just a certain static in the air, nothing more than a feeling, nothing concrete. The bubble of silence broken, and Jeffery was gasping. I thought he was choking, and I rushed for him, arms at the ready to circle his waist, to expel the food from his windpipe. Then, we heard them in the attic, moving our mother's old wardrobe, pushing grandfather's WWII rifle out from behind the broken Singer sewing table, toppling a box of papers down the stairs.

Ghosts, Jeffery said. He knew; somehow, we all did.

As long as they stay up there, Mary said, but of course they didn't. We'd find them in sink drains and behind closet doors and one lodged itself in the overhead light in Jeffery's bedroom where it curled around the bulb, blocking the light. Other ghosts would whoosh toward his bed as shadows danced in the flickering light of the fixture. I can't sleep, Jeffery would say most mornings. I can't sleep at all. He said every time he closed his eyes, he could still see the lights flickering under the shadows of the ghosts.

Light. Dark. Light. Dark.

They crowded into the breadbox and molded themselves onto the English muffins and we choked them down with breakfast, their discorporate bodies expanding in our throats before they seeped out our eyes and swarmed back into the pantry.

It got so bad you'd barely want to close your eyes, Jeffery said once, years after, before his teeth clenched together, his jaw set, and he never spoke of it again, not while he was alive. He wanted to pretend it never happened, and we agreed. Mary and I rarely spoke of it at all, not in front of him and not when he was gone. But one evening, after Jeffery had been dead almost a year, Mary told a story of the night he'd crawled into her bed weeping, and shivered against her and said, *help me, God, they move closer when I close my eyes.*

She'd vowed then to get us out of the house, to escape, or to find a way to exorcise them from our house. But they held us, and we saw them in the edges of our vision. *They move closer when I close my eyes*, Jeffery had said to Mary, these restless spirits who at first might have seemed like lonely visitors just looking for a place to finally find peace.

They froze when we stared at them, but when we closed our eyes, they moved closer and we could feel their tendrils just touching our skin, leaving Arctic trails of fingerprints down our cheeks.

Curious, Mary would say. *They want to know what it's like to be alive.*

Their hands brushed down our backs in the bath, curled into our hair and we'd scream sometimes, but sometimes we didn't, sometimes we'd clamp our tongues between our teeth, blood filling our mouths, imprisoning our voices and we'd pray they'd go away, go back to the attic, move into another home.

We shouldn't have done it, Mary whispered one day because she thought we caused our haunting with what we did to save ourselves.

We should tell someone she added. Mary wanted to call the police or the church or a shelter for abused children. But Jeffery and I were underage and Mary just eighteen. Where would we live? Who would care for us if we couldn't care for each other?

So, we stayed in the house. But the ghosts hid in the living room walls and wrapped around our feet when we walked and after Jeffery sprained his ankle, they got bolder and barely a moment went by when they weren't creeping around, slipping into corners, dancing around the ceiling and the window frames, terrorizing the postman until he would no longer come to the door and he'd leave our mail in a box out on the sidewalk.

Jeffery would run out to get it when he thought the ghosts weren't watching, running down the uneven stones leading from the porch to the street, clutching the mail to his heaving chest to make it back to the heavy oak door before the ghosts knew he was gone. The mail piled on the hall table, like the papers we'd picked up at the bottom of the stairs the day they moved in, old love letters from our father, mostly, and mother's final note.

Escape, Mary whispered one day, and we all went to the door, no suitcases, no money, nothing to make them think we were doing anything but going for the groceries, delivered, like the mail, to the box on the sidewalk, but they knew, somehow, the ghosts, and the doorknob seared Mary's hand. She howled, and we rushed her to the kitchen to run cold water over her burning skin, but the ghosts wrapped around the faucet, and the water froze. Jeffery pulled ice from the deep freeze while Mary screamed and after that, she didn't talk about leaving, not even in a whisper.

Haunt someone else, Mary whispered, day after day. Haunt someone else. *Surely someone deserves this more than us.*

But still they pulled at our hair and sprang from the walls, and we knew we'd simply traded escape from one kind of hell into a different one.

But one day, the ghosts were quiet, and Jeffery didn't wake up screaming in the night. The next, he came back with the mail and a newspaper the mailman had left in the box. The front-page article told of a neighbour who drowned her children in the bathtub.

So bad, Mary whispered, and it was so bad.

Worse than us, Jeffery said, and he was right, for who had we killed, but those who most deserved it?

That night, the ghosts didn't creep into our rooms, they didn't touch us in the bath, they didn't flicker the lights or plunge us into darkness.

For days, for weeks, we listened for them, looked for them. We stared into the mirrors, waiting for our faces to turn into gray, dark-eyed horrors. We trod carefully through the living room, but nothing grabbed our ankles, nothing sprang from the walls.

I think they're gone for good, Mary said one day.

We held our breath for a moment, but nothing happened. They were gone, we realized, though it would be months, maybe years, before we fully believed it. For Jeffery, maybe, they never truly left, and though he wouldn't ever talk about them, we weren't surprised when he eventually left us a note that said he still saw them, still talked to them every day, and then he died, perhaps to join our parents in eternity.

We still don't talk about them much, though Mary writes about them, long novels about haunted houses and dead family members. *I find hope in writing about ghosts,* she says and shrugs as if even she doesn't understand. We look for Jeffery in our own ways—did he find them? Is he one of them now? Is he now haunting someone else, touching their skin, giving them nightmares?

We can't hate them, Mary says, *But I do. I hate them still* and also, she'll sometimes confess, if she's had a cocktail or two and no one else is around, *sometimes,* she whispers, *God help me, I miss them.*

FINNIAN BURNETT

Finnian Burnett teaches creative writing and literature. Their writing explores intersections of identity — fatness, mental health, queer joy. Finnian was shortlisted for the 2023 CBC Nonfiction Prize. Their second novella-in-flash, *The Price of Cookies*, is available from Off Topic Publishing. Finnian lives in BC where they spend their time watching a lot of *Star Trek* and daydreaming about teleportation.

L. N. HUNTER

Friends and Family

You sent me to a lonely death;
I cursed you with my dying breath.
When find you someone you hold dear,
They will not live beyond a year.
While I am hidden deep,
Your dead will never sleep,
And you will endure alone,
'Til your line is naught but bone.
When I am free,
Then you will see;
When it's my turn,
I'll make you burn.

An angry shriek rattled the windows, then the dog hurtled down the stairs and out the kitchen door with a large white bone in his mouth.

"Gran," I shouted up the stairs, "you know you shouldn't tease Mussolini! It's your own fault. I'll get your leg back in a bit, but Cousin John's manifesting in the downstairs bathroom again, and I need to deal with that first."

I've lost track of the number of times I've told her she should wear pants instead of dresses, but her response is always, "I never wore them when I was alive, and I'm damn well not going to start now."

Gran was the first to appear, just before midday. She was always like that: ready and waiting at the door for any occasion at least half an hour early, expecting to be waited on hand and foot—literally only one foot at the moment.

I shooed John out of the house and sprayed some lavender and rosemary in the bathroom. That ought to keep the troublesome good-for-nothing away for a few hours. A glass of milk and a cookie for each calmed the older children he'd frightened with his wailing, but there was little I could do about the dozen crying babies in the front room. There were always so many of them, from long ago when families were big and few children reached adulthood.

I ran across the garden, bellowing, "Mussolini"—it seemed like an amusingly subversive name when he turned up as a puppy but is rather embarrassing now. Two of the boys followed me, Aloysius and Titus, distant cousins who'd died a century or so ago. They thought it was great fun racing through the trees. Foliage passed through them with no more than a swishing sound, while each and every godforsaken branch whipped me on the arms and tangled in my skirt.

By the time we caught up with the dog, he'd started to dig a hole for his treasure. Titus picked up something shiny that Mussolini had unearthed, but I wasn't paying much attention as I snatched Gran's tibia from the dog and inspected it. A bit slobbery here and there but no new scratches—thank goodness.

I trudged back to the house while Titus and Aloysius fought for ownership of their newfound trinket. The squabbling stopped when we arrived back in the kitchen, and the boys noticed the cookies sitting out on the counter. Abandoning their treasure, they grabbed two each and ran off, chasing Mussolini through the house. I picked up the thing they'd dropped and examined it, an obviously very old, but pretty, ring—a simple gold band with *We Join in Love* engraved on the inside. I popped it in my pocket and rushed upstairs to Gran.

She turned her head toward me. Despite it being a fleshless skull, I could tell she was scowling as I wiped Mussolini's drool off her tibia.

She winced when I went to replace it.

"Sorry, Gran." I turned it the right way up and, trying again, slotted it back in with a solid *click*.

I thought about showing her the ring, but she looked so ill-tempered that I decided to leave it until later.

I plodded back downstairs, rolling my neck from side to side to de-crick it. I was exhausted, and it was barely mid-afternoon. It was a relief when Mum faded in at about 4:00pm. She could take care of some of the babies now and keep Gran company.

I'd been up since dawn, cleaning and tidying—I knew what Gran's reaction would be if she detected any hint of dust. I'd also had to pop out to the shops to get food and drink for the visitors. Even though most of them couldn't actually eat or drink, they liked the idea and demanded that there was real food on the table.

I had grown to hate Halloween—it got the spirits totally over-excited. 364 days of the year, they're happy to hide from the world, quietly minding their own business. But this night, they had to be up and about, shouting and moaning and crying and screaming, making my head spin. I mean that metaphorically, not like Auntie Betty who tended to do that as her party trick after a sherry or two.

The house had been in my family for generations, since

before great-great-and-then-some-grandfather Edmund's days. I'd have loved to know more about the history of the place, but he wasn't around to ask about it. I don't mean he'd passed on to *somewhere else*; he was still on Earth. However, unlike the rest, he never turned up on Halloween. Since his time, spirits hung around here, never moving on. The only living bodies in the house were Mussolini and me now.

It was already dark, and gloomy shadows fell across the floor. Somewhere outside, the sun shone, but I could barely see through our windows because of hugely overgrown window boxes, crowded with many generations of scentless ghost flowers. These days, I tried to remember to take a plant out and get rid of it as soon as it showed signs of wilting instead of letting it die in the house.

I disposed of waste vegetables at the local rubbish dump instead of dropping them into our trashcan. *That* was an overflowing cornucopia of translucent lettuces, carrots and other ghostly edibles from before I realized what happened to anything that expired here.

I dreaded to think of the legions of mice, beetles, and other wildlife underneath the house. Fortunately, those phantom creatures were as wary of the light as they were when alive, and kept out of sight.

The doorbell rang, but I ignored it. I knew it would be Ben; he always turned up at this time. When we'd started dating, I thought he was sweet, but after a while, his total unwavering consistency in absolutely everything started to annoy me. He was just so... boring.

Each Halloween, I hoped it would be different, but no. Every October 31st, 4:43 p.m. on the dot, there he'd be, wearing the same spotty bowtie and tweed jacket, holding the same bunch of chrysanthemums, with those same puppy dog eyes staring at me through his big round glasses. I just couldn't face him tonight. I hoped he'd leave if I ignored him for long enough, but I knew full well that he wouldn't.

I heard a brittle conversation start up outside. It sounded like Albert had turned up, too. They met only after they'd both died, but he and Ben never saw eye-to-eye. I listened, and as expected, the voices grew louder and more acrimonious. They'd start fighting if I didn't intervene, but I really just wanted to hide until they went away.

Then Simon arrived. He was the most sensible of my old boyfriends and could pour soothing oil on any situation. I heaved a sigh of relief and hoped that this Halloween would pass at least a little more peacefully than the last few.

Unfortunately, the Dalton twins rolled up in their scratched and dented Dodge 330—it really hadn't done so well for itself at the bottom of the lake. It must be said, the same could be said of the brothers themselves. I'd been dating the boys, James and Jack, at the same time, which was fun until they found out about each other.

Even though they were competing for my heart, they were prepared to combine forces against Ben, Albert and Simon. Brotherly blood, even ghostly, appeared to be thicker than the water they'd drowned in.

It was going to be another Halloween exactly like all the others. The boys fighting outside, Mussolini barking wildly and getting tangled in their legs; Gran and Mum shouting from upstairs windows; Auntie Betty singing rude songs at the top of her voice; the children crying again; and Cousin John sitting on the roof with his pitcher of moonshine, cackling at all this entertainment.

Thank goodness my nearest neighbors were three miles away. I sat down at the kitchen table and put my head in my hands. There was little I could do about the older relatives and the children, but it was my fault that the men were adding to the chaos.

I really wish it hadn't taken me so long to realize that any boy I got serious about died exactly one year after our first meeting. A heart attack had done for Ben. Albert fell while rock-climbing. Lightning struck Simon. And the Daltons—well, the car in the lake... I'd not been on a date for two years, just in case. I couldn't face adding to the collection outside.

The shouting and singing stopped; the world went abruptly silent. Surprised, I stood up, knocking over my chair, but even that toppled soundlessly. I rushed to the door to find everyone looking around in bewilderment. Even Mussolini looked confused, as he barked without making any sound.

A faint whistling built into a rush of air and screamed like a jet engine. Something hurtled towards us from the woods where the dog had run earlier. It resolved itself into a woman in an old-fashioned green dress, flying through the air and shrieking at us. She would have been looked pretty if her face hadn't been twisted in anger.

"Defilers! Vermin, be gone! Leave this place or perish!" The woman landed in front of me and looked me up and down. She patted down loose strands of her long, dark hair, and in a more reasoned tone, added, "Now I think on it, leave or stay, it matters not. You, I will kill, regardless."

I opened my mouth and squeaked. On my second attempt, I managed to ask, "Who are you?"

"I am Lisbeth Wilberforce. Edmund Standish, your ancestor banished me from this place and left me to die—I can smell him on you. Most heartlessly, he imprisoned me deep in the woods. Before the breath left my body on this very day, I cursed him and all who live here, never to leave until I have my revenge." She looked directly at me. "You released me when you removed that ring, the seal on my prison."

"Ring? What ring?" I thought for a moment. *Oh, that ring...*

"Now, I will punish all who descend from Edmund. Even you, girl." Lisbeth reached towards me, but my ex-ex-boyfriends intervened. (All of them, which was sweet, though some of them tripped over the others).

Ben got there first. "Nobody touches her without going through us!"

"Very well." She waved her hand in a complicated pattern, and he vanished with a feeble squelching sound. "Who's next?"

The Daltons had climbed into their car and were thundering towards her. The car buckled on impact, as if it had hit solid concrete. Nonetheless, the crash flung Lisbeth into the air. Frozen, I watched as she landed on her feet and started to gesture again.

However, before she could cast another spell, a new ghost appeared, one I hadn't seen before.

"Lisbeth, my darling!"

The witch froze. "Edmund?"

"Yes, my dearest, how I've missed you." He opened his arms and stepped towards her.

"Missed me?" she laughed. "You *trapped* me—and for that, I will kill you and your entire family."

Now it was Edmund's turn to be taken aback. "Trapped you? Never. No! You vanished on the day I proposed to you. We searched for days but found not a trace."

"You left me to die!" she screeched.

"Mother told me you'd run off with the ring, but I couldn't believe that. I vowed to remain here for your return, even if that meant waiting for eternity."

Lisbeth's eyes widened. "Wait, I cursed you. And your descendants. All of you are only here because of my curse. Why should I do anything but make you burn?"

Edmund looked at her. "Oh, I suppose it *was* easier than I expected to stay here. I did wonder.' He hung his head. 'No

19

matter, I can't go on without you. Do what you will."

Lisbeth raised her arms again.

"Wait!" I shouted. "Maybe Edmund's telling the truth. Does that look like someone who wants to kill you?"

Lisbeth's eyes bored into me.

I gulped and continued, "Could it have been someone else who imprisoned you? Edmond says his mother told him you'd gone—perhaps she knows what happened. If you're such a powerful witch, you should be able to summon her."

She lowered her arms, then closed her eyes and muttered some words I couldn't make out. A shadow faded in and out, eventually forming the outline of a woman.

"Mother!"

"I'm sorry, Edmund," the woman whispered. "I wronged you. I thought she wasn't good enough for you." She turned to Lisbeth. "I feared what spells a witch might cast on my son. But I see now that your love for each other is strong. I wronged you both."

I could see tears in her eyes.

I rummaged in my pocket for the ring and held it out.

Lisbeth deflated, her anger dissolving as Edmund moved to her side and tentatively lifted her hand, placing the ring on her ghostly finger.

"Edmund," Lisbeth whispered, eyes shining. The two spirits embraced and kissed.

Edmund said, "We don't have to wait any longer. We can move on."

Lisbeth looked into Edmund's eyes and smiled. She lifted a hand and spread her fingers. "Now, all can rest."

The couple dissolved into a cloud of sparkles, which floated up into the sky and vanished. The other spirits melted away too, and even the sound of crying babies ceased. All that remained was Cousin John, until he finally vanished with a foul-smelling belch.

It'll be a very quiet Halloween next year.

I wonder if I'll have another boyfriend by then. A living one.

L. N. HUNTER

L.N. Hunter's comic fantasy novel *The Feather and the Lamp* sits alongside works in several anthologies as well as Short Édition's 'Short Circuit' and the 'Horrifying Tales of Wonder' podcast. When not writing, L.N. unwinds in a disorganised home in rural Cambridgeshire, along with two cats and a soulmate.

THERIC JEPSON

The Hunger of Ghosts

My grandmama taught me something about craftsmen. True craftsmen. And craftswomen. *Craftspeople* is probably not a word. *Crafters* is something else entirely. Anyway, you're the writer, not me. And *this* pen I lifted from a roadside motel from a nowhere Nevada town. *Nowhere Nevada town* is not so bad. I've written enough books now to recognize a good phrase. It's necessary because even the best writers still write a crapper now and then.

Anyway. Grandmama's point was that a true craftsman (her word) cares more about the work than the credit or the glory. They just want to keep on working, even after they're dead. Unlike, say, Madam Goldflesh, a famous dancer who grew up round those parts who, according to most accounts, wasn't that skilled or even all that good-looking, but who had such an insatiable need to be seen that we kept on seeing her years after she passed. And then she dissolved because—and here we're getting to my point—she couldn't be tied to an actual physical object. *She* was the point of her life. And she, of course, was dead. Immaterial. Unlasting.

Craftswhatevers are different.

For instance, the shop teacher at my high school was electrocuted holding his hammer. Then, whoever wielded that hammer got nails in one hit, every time. Mr. Smoskowitz was not an ambitious man. But he cared about craft. And his hammer's why Grandmama explained the whole tool thing to me in the first place. It was my idea to get artists involved. My first thought was painters, but even if the painter stayed in the brush, I would still be stuck picking paints. Sculptors: where to place the chisel. Writers, though. All I had to do was clear my mind and keep fresh paper rolling. Ghosts don't tire, of course, so I got a couple Filipina housekeepers trained to give my wrist a break.

Long story short, I end up with five pens. Finding writers still hungry and ambitious as they're dying was the hard part, and I got five! Daisy O'Sullivan, three-time National Book Award finalist. As I type her pen-written manuscripts I just change place names from a cluster in Alberta to a cluster in Idaho. R.R. Krushel, hard-nosed pornographer, in death, tells only stories of sexual regret. He's got me the best critical attention, and all I did was change the three Rs in his name! I don't use the pens of Marta Magwich or Om Mahajan as much because there's no money in short fiction and poetry, but sometimes it's a nice break. I call them both Roxy James. The best though is Todd Kristoph Humm—he won the contract from the Todd Kristoph Humm estate to write new books under the Todd Kristoph Humm name. Each one sells a million or so copies, subsidizes the work of Fleur Irish and N. N. Knushel who move, at best, in the low ten thousands. (Which is pretty great, really, for recluses who don't do publicity. It's a shame their pens don't produce *bon mots* for social media...)

Grandmama herself was a great craftsman, of course, and took great care to die holding nothing. She worried her passions would keep her here forever, sure, but more she worried what someone might apply her passions to.

I am now older than my grandmama was at my birth by the full measure of a decade (is that a good phrase? probably not). I live comfortably in one of those modern glass places in the L.A. hills. I have five ghosts—I thought to do my bidding—but, I realize now, twenty-five years into this life, that I have been doing theirs. And what am I? Who is Charlie Beaumont of Oriole Drive? He who lives alone? Who pays domestics to clean up the messes he does not make and take turns with him holding pens, with a request they learn no more English but knowing they ignore him because their children are now in college and their grandchildren will not speak their grandmothers' language and these women are *alive*. They have seed with whom to speak.

I asked Grandmama once what would happen if she died holding me, but she only laughed, only laughed.

The next morning, as we ate cracked wheat, she said, "Was I not holding your mother, boy?" but I've never been sure what that implied.

Last month, Humm's literary executor emailed a request for books set in the present day. Research shows that the 1980s milieu is the primary reason readers give for slackening interest. But pens don't take notes. And you can't just drop a smartphone into an interrogation scene—it up and changes every interaction. A few years back, I read on a weird-news site of a smartphone found clasped in the hand of a teenager dead of a pulmonary embolism that inexplicably sent contentless snaps to the girl's friends up to her burial. The family buried the phone with her.

In a steel box. Coated in cement

Under six feet of good Wisconsin soil.

Its battery's long dead by now.

I wonder if she still sends her snaps in ignorance.

The problem, you see—the problem with my life, I mean to say—is it has no plot. I do nothing. Risk nothing. Have no secrets to be discovered. Believable secrets, anyway. I tell ghosts' stories, yet I pay no price. They pay me. And their wealth is considerable.

Grandmama warned me against having truck with the dead. They are inherently corrupting, she said. Inherently corrupting. She kept her own communions with the dead limited; she had other work she preferred.

Even now, all these years later, I still think she's wrong. My life may not have produced work of its own. I may not know any living soul well. But I don't blame my writers for this. And I'm not so sure any of those "failures" should count as corruption. Who's to say I wouldn't have been the same without their so-called influence?

Anyway. I didn't realize I was corrupted until this last week, sitting in the mystery section of Barnes and Noble, looking at author photos (priority: young) and bios (priority: near L.A.) Was I actually thinking of getting a pen from someone now alive? Someone who would simply remain alive without my assistance?

Grandmama wasn't much for Jesus, but I've read some Bible in my day and it says something about money corrupting. And I can tell you it's true. I've never killed man nor woman, and I'm not about to start now; I've typed too many crime novels to expect to get away with it.

But I've given my life to five hungry ghosts. What would be one more?

Please destroy this letter regardless, but if you would like to live forever, brain cancer be damned, and you want to sell millions as the new Todd Kristoph Humm, have your loved ones hang some ribbons from the apple tree in your front yard and I'll be in touch.

Yours most sincerely,
        C. Beaumont
        literary preserve

THERIC JEPSON

Theric Jepson is the author of *Byuck* and *Just Julie's Fine*, neither of which feature ghosts. Vigilant busters can, however, find ghosts via close inspection of thmazing.com/thbiblio.

ROB NISBET

Cry in the Night

South Dean, Sussex, U.K. 1995.

Mr. Grigson licked his finger and flicked meticulously through the papers on his clipboard. "So, what do you think?" he asked.

Paul looked around the neglected room. "It's a big job," he said, sucking air through his teeth. "Complicated."

"That's why we want someone to live-in," said Mr. Grigson. "You'd be a sort of caretaker for the building while you worked on the electrics."

"Big building." Paul peered out into the corridor. "What was it? A school?"

Mr. Grigson nodded. "Small local school," he said. "I was a pupil here myself actually, nigh on twenty years ago." He grinned, as if at boyish memories.

"And I noticed some fire damage..." Paul paused.

Mr. Grigson's grin slipped instantly. His reply languished a moment in silence. "There was a fire," he confirmed. "That's why the school was closed. It was all cleared up, but I guess you can't erase something like that completely. Anyway..." He forced a more professional tone into his voice, but his eyes remained troubled, "the council want it converted. It's a prime position for a block of sea-view apartments. So, what do you say? Will you take the job?"

Paul thought of the weeks of lonely work ahead—a couple of months perhaps. But he needed the income, and being this close to the sea would be like being on holiday. He reached for Mr. Grigson's clipboard. "Where do I sign?" he said.

oooooo

Paul moved in a week later. One of the smaller rooms had been furnished with a bed, cupboards for his belongings, a TV and enough provisions to see him through the first few days. He had access to the school kitchen and there were showers next to the gym. It was all quite basic, but he marveled at having so much space. It was like living in his own, personal mansion.

He started work by tracing the electric cables from a gigantic out-of-date fuse box, around the building, marking the walls where sockets and junction boxes needed to be placed. It was a long task and took him well into the evening.

This is the reason they want me to live in, he thought. *Working extra hours with no extra pay.* Eventually, he'd had enough of work and settled to cooking: a jacket potato with cheese and beans. He'd never claimed to be a great chef.

He decided to take a stroll before turning in to bed. He wrapped up against the wind and ventured out onto the sloping grounds towards the cliff top. It was closer than he expected: no fence either. Stupid place to have a school, no wonder it never reopened after the fire. It was too remote, as well, and the road up here had been more ruts than tarmac.

The sea led his eyes out towards a bank of fog that hid the horizon. He walked along the cliff path for a while, but it must have eroded over the years. In several places the path disappeared where a cascade of fallen stones had tumbled down to the rocks and sea below. The sun was getting low in the greying sky and a haze of mist crept closer over the white-peaked waves. Paul decided it would be safer to head back to the school building. This was not the place to be walking in fog or darkness.

He locked the doors and watched an hour or so of TV with only half his attention. It had been a tiring day. He changed into pajama bottoms and a t-shirt, then settled for bed.

It was only with the lights off that the emptiness of the building became apparent. He felt suddenly small and alone. The wide rooms and high ceilings seemed to reverberate with a hollow silence. The sound of his breathing was swallowed up by the darkness, which made the crying more obvious.

Paul strained his ears. Yes, it certainly sounded like crying. Jerking sobs. It definitely wasn't the sea or the gulls.

He switched on the light. The sobs stopped for a moment, then, very faintly, he thought he heard them again, somewhere distant, in another room.

He left a trail of lights on behind him as he traced the sound to what must at one time have been a classroom. The whimpering sobs were definitely coming from inside. It sounded like a child.

Paul pushed open the door and felt inside for the light switch. In the darkness he could see something. It seemed to be a tiny flame: the glow from a lighted match. He strained his eyes. The match was held, he thought, by a young boy, probably about seven years old, just visible in the feeble glow.

Paul switched on the light. The room was bare and silent.

"Where are you?" Paul demanded of the obviously empty room. There was nowhere the boy could be hiding. Paul felt foolish talking to himself. He must have imagined the glow and the shape of the boy's face—perhaps a trick of the moonlight shining through the window. He crossed to the glass panels of a patio door and peered out. No moonlight tonight, a sea fog had curdled the darkness outside. He could see only a few feet at most.

Then a figure stepped towards him out of the fog. A melted face pressed itself against the glass.

Paul leapt backwards, but this was no phantom. A woman shuffled from side to side just beyond the doors, agitated. She stared at him, then peered around him as if searching for something. The features of her face were distorted: red, with a sheen like molten plastic. Her eyes were wide with panic, flicking around the room.

Paul cursed and forced himself forward, fumbling with the door's handle and lock. By the time Paul had the door open, she was gone.

oooooo

The following morning Paul woke fitfully, as if from a bad dream he couldn't quite remember. Then the bizarre incidents of the previous night hit him anew.

He didn't worry about breakfast. He went straight to the classroom where, he was certain, he'd glimpsed a boy in the darkness. On the way, he turned off the lights he'd left on all night. He had closed the door. He took a breath to steel himself and entered the room.

Empty, as before. The fog had cleared, and the new day shone brightly through the windows and the locked patio door. He looked around, but there was nothing to remind him of the night's events. Around the doorway to the corridor he could see evidence that this was one of the fire-damaged rooms. The woodwork had been pared-back and rubbed down, painted, and re-painted, but the signs were still there.

oooooo

Mr. Grigson called round that afternoon, to see if Paul had settled in, and if there were any concerns about the work. *And to see that I am actually working,* thought Paul.

Mr. Grigson seemed happy with the progress so far and ticked a few boxes on his clipboard. Paul offered him a mug of coffee. They took their mugs into the classroom with the patio door. "There's something I wanted to ask you," Paul said. "Last night, I saw a woman, outside that door, looking in at me. She was..." He paused, not sure how to describe her.

"A bit disheveled?" said Mr. Grigson. "With a burnt face?"

"That's her." Paul raised his eyebrows, waiting for the explanation.

Mr. Grigson crossed to the window, hugging his coffee. "That was Anna," he said. "I suppose I should have mentioned her, but she's harmless, and I didn't want to put you off the job. Did I tell you that I had been a pupil here? Anna was my teacher. It was a very small local school, only a few classes, with a wide range of ages up to primary level."

"She was here at the time of the fire?" asked Paul.

"I was only nine at the time," said Mr. Grigson, "and I think they kept some of the details from me. I was at school that day, but I was ill, shivering with a cold, apparently, and there was some problem at the time with the school heating. Anna called my parents to come and collect me. I remember Anna taking me out to Mum's car. The fire was discovered soon after." His eyes drifted, as if trying to focus on something in the past. "I have often wondered if it was because she was out of the class looking after me that she wasn't there to supervise." He shrugged. "It's stupid, I know, but a sense of guilt lingers; it won't rest. I guess I'll never know how, or exactly when, the fire started."

"And her face?" Paul wasn't sure that he wanted to know what had happened.

"So far as I know, the fire started in this room, over there by the door to the corridor. The investigators said that's why the kids couldn't get out. And the teachers, of course, couldn't get in. So, Anna ran round to the patio door from outside, but it was locked. They say the fire had really caught by then. It must have been terrible, whatever Anna saw from outside: a room full of smoke and flames. And the children." Mr. Grigson physically shuddered. "She smashed the windows. It was the raging heat from inside that burnt her arms and face. She couldn't get in. The kids couldn't get out."

"Horrible." Paul shook his head. "You can't imagine anything like that."

"Poor Anna." Mr. Grigson turned from the window. "It was in all the papers at the time. How there should have been more staff. It couldn't happen today, of course. Seventeen kids were lost that day. Practically every family in the village lost a child or knew someone who had. Anna, though, she lost all seventeen. It warped her mind. It's not just her face that's distorted."

"She still lives around here then?"

"Oh yes, she has a small flat above the baker's shop. The village looks after her, and she has carers that see to her needs. Trouble is, she's obsessed by this building. She keeps returning to this window. Looking in, as if she's re-living that day, trying to do things differently."

"Like last night," said Paul.

"Just a theory of mine," said Mr. Grigson, "but I think it's the fog that attracts her. It looks like smoke, you see. She feels compelled to make her way here, look through the window, like she's checking all is well."

Paul ran a hand across his chin. "Makes a sort of sense. I won't be so startled if it happens again."

Mr. Grigson took a sip of his coffee. "We get a lot of sea fog around here," he said.

oooooo

That night a keen wind carried the sound of breaking waves through the school, and froths of sea foam rode the gale outside the windows. The sky, however, was clear. Paul was relieved to see the stars. There was not the slightest hint of fog tonight.

But as soon as he turned off the lights and got into bed, the whispering wind and the sea shared the darkness with the pitiful sound of a child sobbing. He hadn't imagined it, then. What he'd seen the previous night *hadn't* been a mere trick of the moonlight.

He made his way to the fire-damaged classroom, again turning on the lights as he went. The corridor light switch clicked, but no light appeared. Paul cursed, remembering that he'd disconnected this area from a junction box he'd been working on.

The crying continued. There was just enough light for Paul to feel his way to the classroom door and ease it open. As before, a single light glowed, just inside the room. This time he was certain that it was a small flickering match flame. It gave off very little light, but Paul's eyes soon adjusted.

In the feeble glow he could see the face of a boy, young, about seven or eight years old. Gleaming streaks of tears slid down his cheeks, and his head jerked miserably with each sob. Paul made no sound, as he inched through the slightly open door. Even the weak light from further down the corridor threatened to obscure the faint image of the boy with the match.

This is no real boy, Paul reasoned. The boy seemed

strangely insubstantial, only the front of his face showed in the blackness where he was illuminated by the tiny flame.

This was no real match either; it continued to burn far longer than was natural. Between sobs, the boy was breathing on the flame, hopelessly trying to blow out the light, but it stubbornly continued to glow.

Then Paul saw other movements in the black recesses of the room. Distant shapes; again, lit by that single match: other children. It was too dark to see details, but their young faces were turned, grim and accusing, to stare at the boy with the match who sobbed by the doorway.

Near the door, something glinted in the faint moonlight. It lay on the floor. At first Paul thought it was another child, but slowly its outline became clearer. It was metal, a thick tube, chunky at one end. Then he gasped. A paraffin heater. He hadn't seen one for...well, twenty years or so. This one had been knocked over; the fuel glistened across the floor.

That's when Paul realized. "It was you," he said in a whisper. "Playing with matches, while your teacher was out of the room..."

The boy seemed to notice Paul for the first time, and looked up from the flame. Behind him, the room erupted into ghostly blue fire. The children ran, terrified, screaming through the flames, eyes wide, their clothes and hair melting, a black cloud of smoke crept across the ceiling.

Paul watched in horror, and behind him he heard the door swing open, on a breeze perhaps from the wind outside. The swinging door allowed the distant light from the corridor into the room, eclipsing the ghostly fire. The boy, the match and the horror of the burning children were swept away.

oooooo

There was a light mist the following day. It snaked across the grounds in wispy tendrils, and Paul kept a wary eye on the windows of each room he was working in, half expecting a deranged teacher to be peering in at him. He half hoped Mr. Grigson would turn up. Paul wanted to tell him that he'd worked it out.

He had returned to his bed, too shaken to sleep, and pieced together the sequence of events.

The class had been unattended, probably while the teacher took the young Mr. Grigson out to be taken home by his mother. Meanwhile, the boy in the classroom had lit a match.

The knocking over of the paraffin heater, Paul assumed, was an accident. Dangerous things. They wouldn't be allowed anywhere near a school these days. They probably shouldn't have been used back then. Actually, hadn't Mr. Grigson said something about there being a problem with the heating? Perhaps the boy had tried to light the wick. Whatever happened, he felt so responsible for the fire and the deaths of his classmates that he cried every night, a sense of guilt sobbing in the dark, unable to rest.

Then the poor teacher, Anna, had appeared at the window. Paul had glimpsed the terrible scene she must have witnessed. She tried desperately to save her pupils, becoming horribly scarred, both physically and mentally, in the process. It all fit together. Now the boy cried every night, surrounded by his ghostly classmates, forever trying to extinguish that fateful flame.

Paul worked again into the evening. The fog outside had gotten thicker during the day, first obscuring the line of trees at the cliff top, and now, as the sky darkened, it hid everything beyond the windows with a swirling grey curtain.

He had made sure that the classroom's junction box was re-connected and he switched on the light, intending to leave it on all night. He hoped it would have the same effect as before and provide him with a peaceful night with no crying. He was surprised that he no longer feared the boy and his match. Now that he understood what had happened, the ghostly appearance seemed logical and had lost its mystery.

A scream sliced through the air from outside. Faint and distant, not the cry of a child, but of a woman.

The teacher, thought Paul, *Anna*, out there in the dark and the fog, screaming for help!

He unlocked and threw open the patio door, stepping out into the chill blankness of the mist. He could hardly see a thing, and the scream came again, frightened, and from the direction of the cliff.

Blindly, Paul picked his route from memory across the school grounds until he reached the trees. He had his arms stretched out in front of him and he shuffled his feet, feeling for the ground ahead before risking a step too close to the cliff edge.

Another scream told him that Anna was closer now, to the right, somewhere along the cliff path. He could sense the vast openness of the sea to his left and hear the mist-deadened crash of the waves against the rocks below. "I can hear you!" he yelled. "Keep calling!"

He inched his way along the path, then slipped as his foot rolled over loose stones that fell away beneath him. This was hopeless. Another step and he'd have tumbled to his death. "I can't see!" he called.

Instantly, a column of fire flared next to him. It was set back slightly from the path, in the line of trees. It burnt through the mist, a beacon in the darkness. Further along the path another beacon appeared. They were indistinct in the fog, but bright enough to light the path ahead. The cry came again, and Paul didn't think twice. Cautiously he made his way along the edge of the trees, avoiding the eroded gaps where the sea had eaten away at the path. More and more fiery columns appeared, lighting his way, providing just enough light for him to see where he was placing his feet.

Then he reached a ravine, where the path vanished completely in a slide of loose earth. The woman cried out again, a wordless screech of panic. So close! Another beacon of fire flamed into existence at Paul's side, and he peered into the mist over the ravine's edge.

There was Anna, her distorted face turned up towards him, clinging to an outcrop of crumbling rock just below ground level. Paul threw himself flat on the ground and reached down. At his side, the column of fire bent too, leaning over the edge. It was a child, a terrible burning child, casting its light out over the cliff so that Paul could see.

It was a girl. There was a terrible calmness in her face as it flaked and blistered.

Paul reached down. "Grab my arm," he called. And he felt the frantic grasping fingers that clawed into his sleeve. He gripped Anna's arm in return and hauled her up, dragging her over the edge and onto firmer ground.

They clung to each other for a moment, but Paul knew they had to get away from the cliff edge.

The burning girl raised a blistering hand, pointing the way through the fog and blackness of the night, to where the series of beacons lit the way along the cliff top.

Paul eased Anna to her feet and supported her with an arm around her shoulders, following the columns of fire lighting their way. Paul counted the children as he passed them, trying not to see their flaking, blackened faces. He knew already that there would be seventeen. They didn't look frightened, nor happy, just blank as the flames consumed them. Then he reached the last child.

It was the boy with the match, standing at the edge of the trees. Very faintly Paul could see the glow of the school building's windows ahead of him. From here they were safe.

Paul paused at the burning boy, saw the tears drying on his face as his skin crisped and darkened. "Thank you," Paul said. "You did well, you and your friends. Your teacher tried her best to save you, and now you've saved *her*. I'd say you're even." He leant in close to the fire. "No need now to feel so guilty."

The boy and Anna stared at each other. What was left of his eyes locked with hers. It was as if a sense of understanding passed between them. The boy no longer cried, and some of the crazed dread faded from his teacher's face.

The boy looked down at the match still burning in his hand. He drew in a breath and blew. The match flickered and went out, and with it the burning beacons along the cliff vanished too.

ROB NISBET

Rob Nisbet lives in East Sussex UK. He has had approaching 100 stories published in anthologies and magazines. He writes audio drama, having adapted work by Philip K. Dick for radio and having had several audio scripts produced by Big Finish/BBC for their Doctor Who range.

Dark Reflections

"**F**rancie, you look terrible. Have you seen yourself in the mirror lately?" Diane was the epitome of concern, as well as the night cashier at the local MightyMart. She whipped out her compact and held it in front of me, forcing me to see the mirror. Her own hair and makeup were perfect, even at midnight.

The bitch.

I hated that woman for her perfection. Her life hadn't been turned upside down over the past month, haunted by I wasn't sure what. My own reflection's eyes had dark circles surrounding bloodshot whites, deep creases between my eyebrows, and my jaw was clenched so tight it was a wonder I didn't have a mouth full of broken teeth. After one quick glance at the mirror, my eyes dropped to stare at my hands, both twitching slightly as they clenched my open wallet, waiting to pay. Why hadn't the idiot store owners swapped to self checkouts? I wouldn't have to deal with questions that I couldn't and wouldn't answer. Not if I wanted to stay out of the nut-house. No one would believe what had really been happening to me.

"Is it Sam?" Diane dragged my now ex-boyfriend's name out to three syllables.

"We broke up a couple of nights ago." I couldn't risk his life any more. It had been too close the last time. If I died, that was one thing. I couldn't risk Sam or any of my friends.

"And you miss the creep this much?" She finished ringing though two large bottles of rye and shook her head. "He's not worth this much alcohol, honey. I know all about that type. I married enough of them."

"Sam's not a creep. I just haven't been sleeping well, that's all. There's a flu thing going around, I heard."

Diane gave me a knowing smile that said she didn't believe the excuse. But she didn't see a man's face appear in the still open compact mirror, smirking and wriggling his fingers in a sort of wave.

Reggie. My stalker.

He wasn't standing anywhere near us. He was just in the damn mirror. Driving me to drink. My stomach seized up and I fought not to just leave the bottles behind and bolt for the door. I needed the rye to get some sleep, or at least unconsciousness, for a few blessed hours.

The first time I'd seen Reggie had been at Murray's bar. Well, it wasn't the *first* time I'd ever seen Reggie. We had been in the same classroom at school since first grade. Of course, we were such a small town back then that there was only one room per grade in the local schools. The new housing development brought more kids in, but that was when we were in high school. Reggie was still in most of my classes.

This was the first time that he started haunting me. Stalking me.

I sat at the bar nursing a beer and wondering where my boyfriend Sam was. He was an hour late. Not an uncommon thing, but I was pissed that it was happening more and more often. He always had a good reason, but they'd started sounding way more lame lately. I glanced up, looking up at the mirror behind the bar to see the room. Reggie was there, several feet back and slightly to my left. I ignored him, as I always tried to. He was wearing his usual sort of outfit: dark dress pants (never jeans), black loafers with black socks, and a grey button down shirt done up to the neck with no tie.

"Hi, Francie," he said. Reggie's voice always grated like nails on a blackboard to me. "I sure am glad to see you."

"The feeling's not mutual. I'm going out to dinner."

"Another date."

"Yes." I didn't turn to look directly at him, on the theory that if I mostly ignored him he would go away. It had worked at school. Most of the time. Not always. I'd realised after graduation that Reggie had been stalking me since first grade.

"Hey, Francie!" Sam's voice, coming from the entrance, was shaky. "Sorry I'm late. I left in good time, I promise! It was the weirdest thing. Damn near wrecked the truck!"

I swung around on the stool and saw Sam coming toward me, eyes wide and face pale.

"What happened? Were you speeding on the curves by your place again? The town should do something about that road."

"They won't do anything honey. There's not enough traffic to make it worthwhile." Sam said. "I wasn't really hurrying a lot, since I kept getting the sun in the mirrors. Then I saw someone walking in the road, and I hit the ditch a little. Andy came by and pulled me out, or I'd have had to walk in. Couldn't get enough traction to back out on my own. Ground there is pretty mucky, what with all the rain we've been having."

"Who'd be walking on that stretch?" I pushed him into a nearby chair and Murray brought him a draft. Everyone I knew who lived along that road drove, never walked, once they left their own property. Even just to visit one of the neighbors.

Sam drank half of the beer before he answered. "I didn't see who it was, what with the sun. Damn, it was bright. Anyway, there's just a little scrape on the fender, that's all. I can buff it out on the weekend. Not worth bothering the insurance people about."

"Didn't the guy give you a hand?" Murray asked. "His fault, after all."

"No. Didn't see him once I stopped. Must have took off into the trees. Scared that I'd thump him for being an idiot, maybe. Stupid place to walk."

Murray went behind the bar and the other patrons went back to their tables. I looked around, realising that Reggie had vanished. Good riddance.

"Let's go," I said, as Sam finished off the beer. "I'll drive this time."

Two nights later, I saw Reggie again. I'd gone to the MightyMart after a late installation and saw him behind me, mirrored in the window glass as I started to leave with two bulging bags of groceries. I should have kept the cart, but the bags hadn't seemed that heavy when I'd picked them up.

"Hi. Quite the excitement the other night, wasn't it, Francie?" A smirk. God above, I hated that look. I really wished Reggie would leave town or start bothering some other people. Then again, maybe he was and no one wanted to admit it. Like I didn't.

"Yeah."

"See you around, Francie." We reached the door and I waited a moment for him to reach to open the door. He didn't and I turned. No one was behind me. I heard the click of heels from another shopper and that was the only thing that got me moving. I did not want to have any sort of conversation with anyone about what just happened. Or hadn't.

For the next week or so, Reggie appeared at odd times and places. He said a couple of sentences, which I mostly ignored, then vanished. I seriously thought about reporting him to the police to get him some counseling of the physical kind, but since Reggie hadn't actually done anything remotely illegal, I assumed they wouldn't be interested. Besides, I didn't want to give him the satisfaction of knowing that he was weirding me out in a way worse than usual.

I was heading home from Sam's late on Saturday night, about near the place where he said that he'd gone into the ditch. I saw Reggie in my rear-view mirror, lounging in the back seat. I jerked the steering wheel, almost going off the road. I felt the adrenaline rushing through me. *Enough*, I thought, *was enough*.

"What the hell are you playing at, Reggie? I'm getting sick of this shit. How'd you get in my car? I know it was locked."

"I wanted to talk to you, Francie. It's hard to get near you. You keep ignoring me and then walking away." He pouted like a six year old, which is not at all attractive in a grown man.

"I told you that I wasn't interested in talking to you. Or dating you. Ever. Why can't you just leave me alone?" I pulled onto the tiny shoulder and stopped. Reggie was still visible in the mirror but when I turned around to confront him directly, there was no one in the back seat. I stared, forgetting to breathe.

"Be seeing you soon, Francie."

I looked back at the mirror and there he was, smirking. My head whipped around to stare at the back seat with a flash of pain from my neck muscles from moving so fast. There was no one there. He laughed, another teeth-grating sound, and vanished from the mirror.

"He was in the mirror," I kept saying to myself. "He wasn't really here." I checked the doors. They were still locked. "There's no way he could have gotten in or out of the car. He was in the freaking mirror." Between shaking hands and my head oscillating between the mirror and the back seat, it was a long time before I was able to drive.

When I finally got home, the shaking had mostly stopped, but sleep was out of the question. After several rye and Cokes (that were mostly rye, I admit), I was still saying, "he was in the mirror," to myself. I sat in the living room, staring at the nearly empty rye bottle on the coffee table. Eventually I leaned back and gazed out the front window at the shadows of the trees on my front lawn.

The sun woke me as it streamed through the window. Last night's revelation, now seen in the brightness of morning, didn't seem to have the impact it had had in the darkness. I stretched and looked at the level in the rye bottle. "Must have had one too many at Sam's," I said, trying to convince myself that last night was the result of alcohol, not actually Reggie in the mirror. "And since Reggie's been playing his stupid tricks, I thought I saw him in the mirror and I scared myself. That's what happened. That's all that happened." I tried very hard to believe it.

I was brushing my hair about ten minutes later when Reggie appeared behind me. I was looking in the bathroom mirror and there he was. No noise of a door opening or footsteps. I stopped brushing halfway down my hair. And breathing. This could not be happening.

"I'm hurt, Francie," he said, sticking his lower lip out. "You think I'm just a figment of your alcohol consumption. I'm not. I just wanted to talk."

I swung around with the brush at head level and no one was there to connect with. The brush clattered as it left my nerveless fingers and hit the floor. I backed toward the window, so I could see the whole bathroom. It was empty. Just me.

"I'm over here, Francie," Reggie said. I turned slowly back to the mirror and he was smirking again, waving his fingers in his limp hello. He vanished and I sat down on the side of the tub, staring up at the mirror. Where was the damned rye when I needed it most?

I spent the rest of the day removing mirrors, hiding anything vaguely reflective and covering the windows with black matte plastic. Reggie didn't put in an appearance, and by bedtime I felt almost secure. As I set the alarm while on automatic pilot night mode, panic surged. I nearly dropped the damned thing.

I'd forgotten about work. I'd be out with mirrors and open expanses of glass *everywhere*. Reggie could be anywhere. I stared at nothing for hours. Eventually the sun rose and the alarm went off. It took all of my determination to leave the house on time. I couldn't afford to get fired.

Reggie didn't appear for two days. I relaxed. Just a little. That was a serious mistake. When he did return, I was in the car again. Thank God I wasn't on the highway, or I'd have crashed. I'd just turned onto my street.

"You covered all your mirrors at home, Francie." He was pouting. "I might get the impression you don't want me to visit."

"Leave me alone, you creep!" I jammed on the brakes and stopped half off the shoulder, on the grass. "Just go away and leave me alone!"

"I don't want to do that. I like you, Francie. I always did. You should like me. I want you to come away with me. Think about it." He vanished and I started to shake.

The next night Sam and I were at Murray's. Sam was telling everyone about his latest escape.

"It's the weirdest thing," he said. "That's twice now that I've seen some guy walking in the road. Both times in the same friggin place. Weird, eh? At least, I didn't hit the ditch this time."

"Did you recognise him?" Murray asked. "Must be someone who lives nearby, don't you think?"

"Not sure who it might be," Sam admitted. "No one new has moved in that I know of. I was going too fast for a good look. I only really saw him in the side mirror once I'd gone past and you know what those things are like for details."

The nachos I ate felt like lead in my stomach. "You didn't see him in front of you, just in the side mirror?"

"Yeah. Really weird, isn't it?" He snagged the last of the nachos and I let him. Could it be Reggie? Why would he haunt Sam?

"They don't like me," Reggie said, as I walked along the wet streets toward home. "I don't like them either. But you do, Francie. I don't want you to see them anymore. Especially not Sam. I don't like the way he looks at you. He doesn't treat you right. The way I will. Once we're really together."

I saw Reggie reflected in a puddle. I closed my eyes and shuddered. Why hadn't I taken the car? So there'd be no Reggie in the back seat. That was why. There were too many reflective surfaces out in the world to keep him from using something. I clenched my fists and kicked at the puddle, disrupting him and he vanished. "My friends are mine," I said. "I don't have to do what you say."

"You should. I have your best interests at heart." He appeared in a store front window next to a mannequin wearing a tuxedo. It was the wedding store.

"I don't want to see you again." I started running toward the safety of the house and heard laughter from the street behind me. I dropped the keys twice before I managed to open the front door. I slammed it shut and sank to the floor, hands over my ears, so I couldn't hear him. But I did anyway.

"I just wanted to make sure you got home safe." Reggie sounded like he was in the front window. "I care about you, Francie. Good night." He vanished and I spent the night hiding in the closet, sitting and shivering despite the thick duvet I pulled from the bed. Anything to get away from Reggie.

Sam called the next morning. He'd had an accident on the way home, on that twisty road. "I've got a busted collarbone," he said, "and I hit my head on the side post. The truck's in worse shape, but the insurance should cover everything. I just hope they don't hear about me hitting the ditch last week."

"What did you hit? Another car?" My fingers ached from holding the receiver. I tried to stay calm but it was so hard.

"No. Ran off the damn road again. Same friggin place. This time I hit a tree. The left fender and the grill are toast. The alignment might need checking. Just in case."

"Did you see the guy again?" I had to work harder to keep my voice calm and clenched my free hand so that it wouldn't shake.

"I don't remember. The doc at Emerg said I might not."

It had to be Reggie. Sam hadn't had any accidents on that road since he started driving. Ever.

I put the phone down slowly and flexed my hands to relieve the cramps.

Over the next two weeks Reggie appeared whenever I was least expecting him. No one else saw him, which made me wonder how crazy a person could be while still wondering if she was crazy. The house wasn't the sanctuary I hoped and prayed for, since covering the windows and mirrors only meant that I couldn't see him. Nothing could block hearing his screechy laugh. I tried earplugs, but they only mostly worked. Reggie could scream his comments and they were worse than his normal tones.

Sam's questions about my nervous twitches and the evasions about going anywhere with him escalated into a telephone fight, and I told him I never wanted to see him again.

Reggie's laugh echoed in my ears when I slammed the phone down, but I'd rather have Sam alive without me than dead because of Reggie's tricks. Still, the tears didn't stop until I slept. In the closet. Again.

I was sitting in the living room nearly another week later. I'd just shut off the television, turned up loud to drown out Reggie.

Then I heard him humming from somewhere in the house and something snapped deep inside me. I couldn't let this go on. I would be in a nut house if someone saw the inside of my house. *How the hell can I get rid of him? That's what I've got to figure out,* I thought. *There has to be a way. And it's probably at his place.*

I had never been to Reggie's house before, but I knew where it was. Reggie hadn't had to move out, unlike the rest of our class. His parents were both dead: his dad when we'd been in fifth grade and his mom the year we'd graduated. I pulled up and stared at the house. Some flowers and weeds under the windows, Reggie's beater car, inherited from his mom, in the side driveway. No sign of anything seriously wrong, but the curtains were drawn and the lawn was getting out of control. All signs that no one had been home for a while. That didn't make much sense, but nothing about what was going on at the moment did. I wondered if anyone would ever believe this living nightmare. I took a deep breath.

I parked down the street slightly and went to the back door, my tool belt a comforting weight around my waist. The door was locked, but as usual in this area, there was a key under the mat.

I closed the door behind me and looked around the kitchen. The house smelled musty and there were dirty pots in the sink and a plate and such on the table. I started to go into the living room, but stopped and went back to the table. I peered at it with a sliver of light from the flashlight. The plate was furry with mold. What the heck?

Reggie couldn't be living here. Then where was he? I wiped my palms on my jeans and took a couple of shallow breaths, trying for calm. As usual, it didn't really work. Was coming here even a good idea?

The light shining in from the street lamp was barely enough to see the living room. The big flashlight on my hip was reassuring, but I didn't want to use it again unless necessary. God knew, I didn't want to attract the cops' attention and try to explain what I was doing here.

Reggie's body was in the basement.

I knew as soon as I walked near the basement door that something had died down there.

The only light seemed to be a string-pull bulb at the base of the stairs. Old, stupid system. Reggie hadn't managed to turn it on. My stomach heaved and I clamped a hand over my mouth to keep from retching as the air currents brought more of the stench of death toward me. I sat down on the top step.

The shakes came back, so I had to use both hands to shine the flashlight down the stairs. I saw his body sprawled at the bottom. There was a mirror near him, an old one in a stand, angled down as if looking at the body. It reflected Reggie's body, his arm stretched toward it.

"Why did you come, Francie?" Reggie asked from the kitchen window. "I don't want you here."

"You're dead, Reggie. I'm looking at your body. Why are you still here talking to me?"

"Shut that door, Francie. Come into the living room. We'll talk there."

"That's the mirror you really need," I said, hoping it was true. It was the only thing I could think of that fit. I was amazed that I *could* think. My hands had almost stopped shaking, but I didn't want to move. Didn't think I could move. Not just yet.

"Come away from there. Those stairs are dangerous, Francie." Reggie's tone was sharp, commanding. So unlike his normal demeanor. "Come into the living room, and we'll talk."

I took a deep breath. I stood and started down the stairs, instead, testing each step. There was a cracked one about halfway down. "That must have been why you fell," I said. The one above it groaned, and I quickly moved to a lower step, gripping tightly to the handrail. It didn't seem very sturdy either, but it was that or maybe fall and land on...

"Get back up here," Reggie ordered. Still that sharp tone. Then he appeared in the mirror in the basement, reflected above his body. "Leave it alone, Francie. You can't do anything down here."

"You can't get out of the mirror, Reggie. You can only frighten people from inside a mirror. You can't come out and *do* anything. That's why Sam only saw you in his mirrors. You distracted him and that's all you could do." I prayed that it was the truth. I would go to church every Sunday for the rest of my life if I survived this. The last few steps were hard to take. I didn't want to be anywhere near Reggie or the damned mirror.

I moved to the side of the body, trying to breathe through my mouth, so I couldn't smell it. The temperature was cool down here, but the body had started to rot.

Reggie was furious at me. "I *can* come out, Francie," he said. "I'll show you." His reflection blurred and something luminous started to come out of the mirror toward me.

I dropped the flashlight and it rolled to one side, thankfully still pointing toward the body. I ducked below whatever was coming from the mirror and headed into the darker part of the basement.

"Where are you, Francie?" Reggie's voice was different, strained. The thing coming out of the mirror glowed in the dim light. It almost looked like an arm, fingers extended an impossible length. "I'll bring you in here. With me. That way we can be together forever. I've always loved you, Francie. Ever since we met at school. Come to me."

My hand reached for the tool belt and slid the hammer free. Now, I gone beyond frightened into anger. I was really pissed off and pumped with adrenaline. I didn't really think about what I was doing. It just happened.

The hammer left my hand and sailed into the mirror, shattering it into thousands of pieces. I turned my face away from any flying splinters and heard a shrill keening.

When I managed to look back, I saw bits of Reggie in the shards, fading from sight. In one piece, his mouth opened in a silent scream. With hands that gradually stopped trembling, I picked the flashlight and stared at the shards until nothing else was reflected in them.

I was safe now. I hoped.

LEE F. PATRICK

Lee F. Patrick is a Calgary author writing mostly SF and Fantasy. Lee has published five novels in three different series (Coalition of Shifters, Mind Games, and Assassins Justice) along with various short stories and Celtic style poems. Lee is on Facebook as @LeeFPatrick. Books are available through various venues.

ALIX KELINDA

A Memory of Colour

A ruthless bone-coloured sun beat down upon the onyx plain. Maxwell's skin was blistered with raised dots the colour of gunsmoke. His lungs ached. His eyes stung. Still, he pressed onward, adjusting his Sillitoe tartan kerchief higher upon his nose and gripping his satchel tighter.

A soft rustle caused him to spin around. There was only cracked earth dotted with scraggly vegetation as pale as eggshells and empty streambeds longing for rain. In the distance, charcoal mountains were eroding into sloping pediments and lonely spires. Occasionally he would spot an echo of what these prairies had once contained, a piece of corrugated sheet metal or a single steel blade from a collapsed wind turbine, but for the most part, this once-busy and once-lush land had been picked clean during The Vanishment, pillaged and then abandoned.

Maxwell scanned his surroundings but saw nothing of

consequence. What was he expecting? No one sane ventured across this unforgiving terrain. Turning around, he wondered what that said about him.

His boots crunched over a patch of ashy, brittle grass, which had once swept green across unending grasslands. A single drop of sweat slithered down his brow. He wished he could break out into a proper sweat, but the air was too dry, and his body wasn't in the habit of wasting water.

A flash of movement.

Whirling in its direction, he saw only stillness. Yet he could have sworn he'd seen... *something*, like a shadow dashing across the plain. He closed his eyes and pressed fingers into his temple. Rumours of desert psychosis had made their way across the ever-more-northerly-shifting parallel that separated this barren landscape from liveable earth. Excessive exposure to the sight of this anemic wasteland could drive any person mad. Maxwell needed to return home before these rumours caught up with his reality.

Home. Where a muted sky blue might be glimpsed. Not a vibrant blue, naturally, but a dash of something other than these melancholy hues. His chest ached at the thought, and his head shrieked with longing.

Dropping to his knees, Maxwell scrambled to open his satchel, desperate to admire again what had brought him to this dreary territory. Flipping over the well-worn flap, he peered inside, squinting at first, the way a person used to when they'd step outside a dark basement and into the sun. Before the sun's resplendent rays turned matte and pale.

The neons disappeared first. Flickering green lights were suddenly as grey and dull as the signs they were mounted to. Soon after, the pastels turned ashen. Primary colours faded. Food blanched and no longer sated. Cerulean bodies of water morphed into chalky liquids that failed to quench a thirst.

But this... this was a relic from The Before.

Maxwell stared into his bag and found he breathed a touch easier. Pieces of himself, pieces he feared he was losing, seemed to slot back into place, the colour restoring his sanity. He licked his lips. Saliva pooled in the floor of his mouth. What might this treasure teach his tongue if he were to tear away its peel and suck it dry?

The idea of handing this luminous fruit to his son and watching his eyes go round with wonder stopped him. His wife would be standing by in her sand-stained dress, a hand pressed to her heart, tears welling in her eyes but refusing to fall, to be wasted on sentiment. He must bring this prize home to his family. They would taste it together. Bury the seeds in their backyard, protected by fences and shielded from the unquenchable appetites of others. They would pour every spare cup of water, every drop of their own sweat if they had to, onto the charcoal soil and pray it would sprout up a new shade, a new hope. That was why Maxwell was here. That was why he had hiked across broken and bleak plains until his eyes bled from the colourlessness.

Footsteps.

Maxwell slapped shut the flap and leapt upright.

A small figure stood mere meters away. Certain he was going mad, Maxwell blinked twice, three times, four, before the figure came into indisputable focus. It was a boy wearing a long-sleeved white shirt and knee-length shorts with black socks pulled high.

Maxwell's first instinct was to worry for the child. "Are you alone? It isn't safe out here." But as he took in the cleanliness of the boy's shirt and the plumpness of his cheeks, his concern diminished. This child, wherever he'd come from, was clearly better cared for and better fed than anyone back home. He bit back the image of his own son, whose sharp bones jutted out from weather-worn skin.

The boy stepped closer. His complexion was smooth and whisper-white, except where the hollows under his eyes were shaded an unflattering sooty black.

"Are you lost, son?"

"Not in the least."

The boy's airy reply ruffled Maxwell. "Well, best be on your way, then."

"I think not."

"These parts aren't safe for a young lad."

The boy only raised his chin. His movements gave the impression of a dog seeking to better sniff the air.

"Do as you will, then. But I must carry on."

Maxwell tossed the strap of his bag over his shoulder and turned his back to the child. He wasn't afraid—not yet. He was a sizeable man, if somewhat haggard from his journey. The boy couldn't be more than seven or eight, couldn't weigh more than seventy pounds. So he wasn't afraid. He walked on, listening for following footsteps—without fearing those footsteps—and hearing none.

"You are carrying something."

Maxwell jerked to find the child directly beside him. "How did you—? Never mind. Be gone, will you? I'm on an important mission and cannot be delayed." He quickened to a brisk walk. The boy followed, keeping pace despite the considerable difference in their leg lengths.

"You are carrying something," the boy repeated.

"What I carry is no concern of yours."

"It's yellow."

The first of many hairs straightened on the back of Maxwell's neck. "Adding spying to your list of unfavourable qualities, eh, son?"

"I don't have anything yellow."

"Neither do I. No one does."

"There's no need to lie."

"Don't be daft," Maxwell grumbled, further lengthening his stride.

"Would you share it with me?"

Maxwell couldn't understand how the boy was still beside him. His own breathing was growing laboured from the vigorous pace while the child appeared unaffected.

"I can't share what I don't possess."

"Come on now, please," the boy carried on, his voice light. "I don't have any yellow. I have blue. And I have red. But yellow—"

Maxwell stopped and barked, "Be gone!"

Except he was shouting at no one, as if his cry had been a spell enacted.

He closed his eyes and pushed knuckles into his forehead, attempting to massage away the delusions. No one ventured across these lands. No one sane. The thought wiggled around his mind like maggots upon rotting flesh. He'd been out here too long. He needed to focus on the hum of life inside his satchel. Needed to focus on his mission. On his son. His family. His home.

He re-opened his eyes. The boy was directly in front of him. Maxwell stumbled backward.

The boy stared. His obsidian eyes seemed to contain no pupils and his lids never met in a blink. "I have been patient, but I require your yellow."

Fear scratched down Maxwell's spine as he tightened his grip on his bag.

"Your yellow." The child outstretched his hand.

"You can't have it," Maxwell hissed. "I found it. It's mine."

"Mine." The boy spoke plainly but his eyes burned like charred embers. "Mine. Mine. Mine. It's a familiar story. One I have heard many times. Do you think you are the first to deny my request?"

Maxwell went to step around the boy, but no sooner had he shuffled sideways than the child was in front of him, drifting effortlessly by way of air and apparent devilry. "Get away from me, you... you creature!"

"You will give me what I need."

Maxwell wrenched his satchel further out of reach. "I will not hand over what is rightfully mine."

"Mine." This time the boy seethed the word, his voice lowered to an octave more befitting the growl of a bear. Loose dirt rose around him, carried upward by a gust of wind.

Maxwell lurched away.

The boy spun so quickly he appeared as nothing more than dust until he reformed as a person on Maxwell's right. Maxwell staggered to his left.

"I will defend myself!"

"Do you think my blue and red came easily?" Again he misted and reformed on Maxwell's other side. It was a taunt, a threat, a demonstration of witchcraft Maxwell could not begin to comprehend. His teeth chattered as if the desert heat had given way to the chill of a sudden sunset. The boy swirled around him as unfathomable particles. Maxwell stumbled in circles, his neck swiveling, whiplashing, until the child coalesced before him.

"I give you a choice, *sir*." He spoke the honorific with condescension. "To repeat the past. Or to do as you should." He thrust out his hand. "Your yellow."

Blood thrummed in Maxwell's ears. He thought of spectres. Of vengeful spirits. Of childhood tales told over campfires long-gone. Of desert psychosis. Of lemons. His treasure. Ripe and golden and belonging to him. He thought of his son. A tree growing in their backyard. And Maxwell made his choice.

He broke into a sprint. He dashed over splintered ground and wilted shrubs. A tornado of ash and bone swirled alongside him, wind whipping at his hair and tossing dust into his eyes. Maxwell changed direction. He dodged skeletal trees and leapt over deep crevices. Still, he could not outrun the hurricane that was a child dismembered. He picked up speed, finding untapped reserves that seemed to spring from his conviction. His lungs screamed. His legs burned. His vision saw nothing but whirling greys, dirt sprayed in every direction. Until all at once, the particles snapped together right on top of him and sent him soaring.

He sailed, weightless, for the distorted length of a dream. Then he landed on his back with a thud and a crack, unable to breathe. Still, he clutched his satchel, knuckles white and unyielding.

"You cannot have it! It's mine."

"How predictable you are."

The boy stomped a foot on Maxwell's chest. Maxwell writhed helplessly and coughed up oily blood. His head hammered, unable to process how someone, some *thing*, so small could be so strong.

Maxwell tried to hold the satchel's flap shut. The boy simply grabbed his wrist and twisted it backward. Maxwell heard the snap before he felt the pain. He howled.

The boy snatched the satchel from his useless grasp. He dug into the bag and liberated Maxwell's treasure-no-longer. His eyes shone like glass as they reflected back the lemon's radiance.

"Yellow." He spoke in awe.

A tear leaked from Maxwell's eye. What a waste, he thought. He stared up from the ground at an incomprehensible power.

Before Maxwell could lament his loss to the skies, the boy

was moving again. He whirled and spun. A cyclone growing wider, swirling faster. Except this time, instead of scattering particles of ash, he released droplets of... Maxwell blinked, twice, three times... droplets of colour. Red and blue and yellow. And... green. Greens. Their lost hues were springing up everywhere. Olive and seafoam and emerald. The windstorm was an artist painting the world anew.

Maxwell's eyes stung from the brightness, yet he couldn't look away. Colour. There was *colour*. The single shades so many men had horded like wealth were now combining into an endless spectrum.

As blood spilled from his lips and his chest caved in, Maxwell sputtered a laugh. He laughed at the unparalleled beauty. At the foolishness of greed. At the joy this revitalization would bring to his son—so much more than a single tree planted behind a spiked fence.

Then again, maybe Maxwell laughed simply because he'd been out here for too long.

ALIX KELINDA

Alix has an undergraduate degree in Psychology, a master's degree in Medical Sciences, and a certificate in Creative Writing. She won second place in the 2019 Robyn Herrington Short Story Contest (published in *In Places Between*) and has a chapbook published by Radical Bookshop (2021).

KAITLYN PETRY

The Tale
of the
Necrobotanist

There are long, winding trails through the dark forest. Undergrowth cut back, trees removed, dangers abated. This is not one of those trails.

The locals pointed it out: *take the western path, the one behind the apothecary. You'll pass a tree cleaved in twain, a still pond, a fox den.* Jaime finds it only because it's marked. Scuffs in the grass, a sign nailed to a tree, "Do not enter."

The trees barely part here, the barest hint of an old path thick with new growth. The closeness of the brambles doesn't deter Jaime. They're an adventurer, after all. Wading through the dense thicket, their sword hews twisted limbs with ease, leather bracers deflecting the skeletal branches clawing for fabric and hair.

Moving further into deepening darkness, Jaime reflects on the circumstances that brought them first to the village and then to this trail.

A series of disturbing tales barely overheard at the neighbouring tavern. Snippets caught over the drinking of wizards, the snapping of fighters, the laughter of bards and the brooding of rogues. Sitting alone in the busy tavern, nursing an ale as amber-brown as their eyes, Jaime had listened and observed, well accustomed to picking up jobs by piecing together others' stories. One can't wait around for a local to ask for help or approach a guild to see what's posted—not when they're considered 'a little bit odd'.

So, they listened. According to talk, a handful of ill-fated companions had failed to return from a once-sleepy village. Despite an interest in gossiping, none of the other adventurers seemed keen to go looking for the missing.

But Jaime was plenty keen. Keen to be away from the crowded taverns, the choked roads, the busy paths. Keen to be away from the quest givers and the innkeepers, tavern loiterers, and inquisitive locals. It was too loud, too busy, and expectations loomed over everything. Expectations on how to dress. How to act. What to say. *"You must curtsey, darling. You must sit with your ankles crossed, like so."* You must never wear anything too comfortable OR too revealing. You must look at a man one way and not another. Not like an equal, never that. You must keep your hands soft. Your fingers slender for needlework. Your chin tilted down. Take up only approved hobbies. Growing flowers. Painting pictures. Reading books.

Jaime only like books about knights. Only liked growing flowers with thorns.

When you're a loner, you must be willing to do what others will not. So, Jaime set upon the road to the village with no companions to wrangle and no opinions but their own to juggle.

They arrived in the village to the sight and smell of picked-over bodies in the streets. Homes were crudely barricaded, boards scavenged from the carts that would have taken goods to market, stalls that would have stood in the village square, and fences that would have kept the wolves at bay. Eerily quiet, it smelled like burnt and rotting flesh. A strange smell beneath that, a loamy, earthy smell: freshly-turned dirt in the garden, damp, crushed grass, and morning petrichor.

Several villagers congregated within an old stone temple, grown over with vines and moss, its stones cracked with nature's attempt at reclamation. There, the tavern whispers were confirmed. Each night, the town was overrun with shambling skeletons held together by vines. Skeletons that moved with ease, as though their musculature was still intact. Regrown. The villagers had a tale to tell—a terrible power lived in the woods. A warlock. A powerful necrobotanist.

A what?

A necrobotanist.

Intrigued, if incredulous, Jaime accepted the directions. *Take the western path, the one behind the apothecary, you'll pass a tree cleaved in twain, a still pond, a fox den.*

Plunging through the undergrowth, they come upon the tree first. Struck by lightning, by the looks of the charcoal striations.

The pond next. The ground dips below the path and softly cups a pool of still rainwater like a hand raised to a mouth, ready to drink.

The fox den is dug from the rotting corpse of a fallen tree. Jaime waits quietly, but there are no sounds from within. Further down the trail, it becomes apparent what happened to the fox. As broken as the tree, its parts now a home for wriggling maggots.

Having run out of instructions and unsure of where to go next, Jaime listens to the woods. The air below the canopy is still and heavy, weighed down by condensation. Beneath the stillness, there are bird sounds, faint and far. Beyond that, the sound of rustling leaves, snapping twigs, softly churning undergrowth—worms and centipedes crawling through the dirt and the dry fallen leaves, spiders spinning their webs.

A loud snap. A shift. A breaking open of the earth. Jaime clutches the hilt of their blade and moves toward the sound. Noises have never frightened them. Things that made others nervous—darkness, loneliness, differences—are all familiar.

They break through the brush into a clearing. The canopy is intact above, but the trees seem to have bowed around this patch of earth, enfolding it in a circle and hiding it from the path. Protecting it. A quick scan of the clearing paints a small rise of earth upon which a cairn of stacked, white stones marks what can only be a grave. A dense hedge of thorny brambles circles the rise, and across the path, a fallen tree is splayed, its rotting contents open to the sky, a patch of strangely mottled growths freckle its craggy surface.

The clearing is washed in the colour of a rosy sunset. Pink that breaks through clouds and canopy to dapple the cool, dark shade. The shade deepens to impenetrable darkness at the other end of the clearing. Something snaps behind them. Jaime turns and finds the forest they've just traversed as dark and foreboding as the woods on the other side of the cairn. Night reclaimed it while they hesitated on the edge of dread.

They step backward two paces into the pink light of the clearing and stop. Sticks snap. Leaves and brush rustle. Just a moment ago, the forest was still enough they could hear the spiders in their webs, but out of nowhere, a cacophony of sound erupts. Creaking, groaning, breaking and slithering.

Jaime takes another backward step, sword raised, and their foot crunches something, a firm texture that gives way beneath the pressure. Their booted foot sinks into the rotted tree, and as it does, it crushes several of the strangely mottled mushrooms, releasing a gaseous odour that makes them cough. Reflexively, they open their mouth and suck in more of the fetid air, breathing in the sour-smelling swamp. Lungs revolting, they cough harder until doubled over. The twig snapping pauses for a moment, then begins again, closer. When Jaime pulls their arm back from across their mouth, there are splotches of red on the brown sleeve. Jaime staggers further into the clearing, unsure of where to go, where might be safe to fall to their knees while struggling for air. Their failing vision lands on the rise of dirt and the stone cairn upon it— just as it moves.

oooooo

Swollen, heavy eyelids part. Above, a dark, starry sky is blotted in irregular shapes by the shifting tree canopy. At first, it seems like the sky is moving, like a child's spinning top. But the sky isn't the one moving.

With this realization, Jaime becomes aware of sensations. The ground moving beneath their back, soft and moss-covered, dampening their clothes. The occasional twig grabbing and scratching at their arms, whipping across the exposed skin at the nape of their neck. Something is wrapped under Jaime's arms, some kind of rope drags them across the clearing. Jaime bucks and squirms, but they're weak. Already spent. It feels like a blacksmith is trying to hammer out a dent in their chest piece. Their lungs fill in short huffs and expel in time with the rapidly increasing thrum of their heartbeat.

Struggling weakly at the end of the tether, Jaime is unceremoniously dropped. The rope, which is not a rope, starts to unravel — vines. Long, leafy tendrils untwist themselves as they recede. Jaime thrashes against them, finally breaking free enough to push into a sitting position and scrabble a few feet across the mossy, damp earth before taking full stock of their surroundings.

It's fully dark in the clearing now. The cairn and the small hill are directly in front of where they've been deposited, dragged around the perimeter of the bramble hedge. A sliver of moonlight gleams against the rounded shapes of the mound, casting it in a pale blue glow. Jaime squints into the dim light, suddenly able to make out darker shapes in the white. Eye sockets. The upside-down leaf of a hollow nose. The cairn isn't rocks, it's skulls.

That's when they notice a glint of moonlight off burnished silver armour. Letting out a strangled cough, Jaime takes in the bodies of the missing adventurers caught against the side of the thorny hedge. Dead, empty eyes look out of rotting faces, thorny red vines snake out of noses and mouths.

"Why did you come here?"

Jaime whirls toward the voice, but there's no one there. Just the small rise of earth and the grisly cairn.

"To... help the villagers."

"To help the villagers," scoffs the voice, mocking.

There's a long pause, then laughter seems to fill the clearing from every direction. Jaime's head swivels, just within the tree line, dark shapes move, skeletal figures creak and shake as laughter rises from rotted bellies.

Jaime presses on, cutting through the sound. "The villagers sent me here in search of a powerful necrobotanist..."

"A necrobotanist!" The voice ratchets up, the laughs emboldened.

"The...skulls...and the vines...the creatures..." Jaime coughs and sputters, defensive.

"Necrobotanist. Ridiculous."

"Then what are you?" Jaime asks.

"I was a druid." The skull at the top of the cairn swivels slowly until its empty eye sockets come to regard the adventurer below. "I once made my home in these woods. I traded with the village. I called myself one of them for a time."

"And now?"

"Now I'm dead." If a voice could contain a shrug or a look of derision, this one would. "Obviously."

Jaime's planned retort dissolves into furious coughing. They struggle to their hands and knees.

"Soon, you'll join me," the voice adds softly.

Standing, swaying, Jaime wipes their mouth on the back of a dirty sleeve, beginning to unbuckle heavy armour. The iron drops to the mossy earth with a clang, and they suck in a satisfying breath laced with rot and decay. Stepping away from the cairn, they search for a trail in the muck.

"Stay!" the voice surges forward, echoing around the edge of the clearing. "Stay for a while longer." And more softly, "At least until the end."

"I would rather die in the den with the fox." The adventurer spits red.

"Please?" the voice asks.

Jaime turns back, regarding the cairn with eyes like dark honey. "Why?"

"You were the first one who didn't say they'd come to kill me."

The adventurer shrugs, wiping their mouth again, ignoring the red on their sleeve. "Doesn't mean I won't or can't."

"Is there no alternative?"

"I don't know," Jaime shrugs. "Talk?"

"Fine," the hollow voice says. "Let's talk."

Jaime glances toward the woods, avoiding the sight of the bramble hedge with its grisly fortification. There's no home for them beyond the darkness. No one they'd like to see before they go. No voice they'd like to hear before they die. No warm bed they'd like to lie in before they rot.

Shrugging, they climb the rise of dirt towards the cairn. The stones at the base can be distinguished this close, a small foundation beneath the stack of three bleached skulls. There's no inscription, no adornment. Next to it, Jaime finds a spot to settle where it's relatively dry, and the moss is soft and comfortable.

"So why all this?" they cough, motioning around the clearing.

"Why not?" the voice asks flippantly.

"Do you need lifeblood to sustain your magics? Do you crave destruction to sate your vengeance?"

"Vengeance?" the voice barks, then softens. "No, not vengeance."

"Then why?"

"I said I used to live among the villagers," the voice continues as Jaime softens into the ground, body slackening as they recline. "I was different. Strange to them. I was an outsider."

Brown eyes reflect the dark sky, memories there, in the shape of the clouds that pass before the stars. A child who sits alone. Who belongs nowhere. Not in their home with their family, not in the clothes they are forced to wear, not even in their own body.

"Is that why you left?" Jaime whispers.

"I came to live in the forest for a time."

"But?"

"They pursued me. The villagers. Constantly tormenting me. The children threw rocks through my windows, the adults knocked over my cart and murdered my chickens. They dug up my plants and trampled my garden."

"That's awful," Jaime murmurs, thinking of the child in the

memories, knocked to the ground, dirt ground into their palms until they bled.

"People are awful," says the voice, thoughtful, as though regarding them.

"So when you died, you became the necrobotanist? To exact vengeance?"

"No. When I died, the villagers dug up my grave and separated my bones. Trapping me here."

"And then the vengeance?"

"NOT YET!" The voice shakes the clearing, stones skittering away from the base of the cairn.

"Go on then," Jaime prompts weakly.

"I communed with the forest for many years," continues the necrobotanist. "Beyond my influence, the village grew and dwindled and grew again. Through my friend the fox, I watched from afar. Through my friend the hawk, I looked on. But the villagers trained the hawk. They killed the fox. I was completely, utterly alone."

"How long?" Jaime asks.

"Ten years? Or a hundred."

"Then why all this, why now?" They indicate the skeletal figures surrounding the clearing, the bones and the bodies and the rot.

The voice does not respond. In the silence, Jaime looks up at the small window of the night sky visible through the canopy, now beginning to lighten due east, still glinting with stars. Pinpricks in the curtain of the dark. They press their fingers into the loamy, soft earth. Their heart is beating slower now, and their shallow, small breaths are slower too. There's a glimmer at the edge of their vision, and Jaime turns their head slightly. A tall, shimmering figure stands beside them. Light blue, the colour of the skull in the moonlight. The slender figure is clad in cropped trousers and a tunic lashed at the waist, long braided hair swept over their shoulder to reveal the high bones of their face, sharp like cut glass.

"You..." Jaime's words hitch with their breath, "...were lonely?"

The figure nods. The canopy overhead shifts, blocking the moonbeams and casting the clearing into deeper darkness. The voice, when it speaks, comes from every direction. "The world spins, and I am frozen to this spot. I can't move my feet, and my arms reach only a small circle around me. I try to reach for the world, but there's nothing to grasp. Around me, it's changing too quickly. The ground is eroding, and I can never find purchase. I pull grass out of the earth, dig into the dirt. When there's nothing else to hold, I dig into my own flesh. With the pain comes numbness. For a time, I feel nothing. I want nothing. I am nothing. And that is worse than wanting the world."

Jaime watches the sky turn above them. Their eyes flutter closed as nausea rises with the spinning of their vision.

"The forest wants to help me," the necrobotanist continues. " It grows closer, slowly. It reaches out its branches, boughs, and vines until I have something to hold."

Vines snake around Jaime's arms, anchoring them to the earth and pulling them down against the loam.

"The world slows its spin. I am aware of time again. I am aware of my emptiness. My unimportance. The world has abandoned me. Moved on without me. Forgotten me. At first, I want nothing to do with it. I remember moments of happiness, and the longing betrays me. Soon, I am nothing but grief. The anguish of being just as alone now as I was when I was a living thing."

Taking slow breaths, Jaime is quiet for long enough to notice the rotation of the night sky. The circling of the stars is like a pod of sharks around a speck of blood. The vines tighten slowly, pulling at them slowly, so they hardly notice themselves becoming one with the brambles and the moss. "I have also been alone," they say. "For a very long time."

A breeze moves through the canopy, and the trees bend away from the clearing, opening up the view of the sky to reveal the full breadth of the stars above, so many, they are vastly beyond count. Not a pod of sharks, but a whole, boundless ocean. A salty tear traverses the short band of flesh from Jaime's eye to their ear and collects along the highest bone of their cheek before soaking into the earth. The vines shiver with hesitation and, after a long moment, begin to retract.

"Here," the necrobotanist urges. "Look."

Jaime's head turns, watching as a small green plant struggles from the dirt. It pushes through the closely woven grass and thick moss until they take pity. Rolling onto one side and shaking the vines free, they gently help the little plant emerge. Once it's grown a few fingers tall, the plant blossoms into a delicate purple flower.

"Eat," the voice says. "And I'll tell you how to save the village."

Jaime regards the flower for only a moment before doing as they're bidden, plucking it and biting it from the stem. It grinds between their teeth, releasing a sweet, grassy taste that soothes their aching throat and flavours each deepening breath. They plant their hands in the moss and sit up, shifting to their knees and then to their feet. When no more vines ensnare them, no skeletons appear in the murky shadows, their eyebrows knit together in confusion.

"You're free to go," says the voice.

"The village?" Jaime asks, cradling their ribs with one arm while the other hand hovers by their empty scabbard.

"I do not need it," the voice says before Jaime can turn

away, "as long as you return, willingly."

Jaime regards the cairn. Its stack of bleached skulls and nondescript stones now glows faintly with the first red light of dawn. It's trapped here, like its occupant, amid the circle of brambles and the bones of the many who had come to strike it down and failed. *Not all problems can be vanquished with a sword*, they think. *Not all different things are the monsters they appear to be.*

They consider a moment, and nod, before turning back to the still, dark woods of the empty forest.

Later, in the tavern, Jaime tells their story. And around them, a crowd gathers to listen. *There are long, winding tales about bright, sun-dappled forests. Undergrowth cut back, trees removed, dangers abated.*

This is not one of those tales

KAITLYN PETRY

Kaitlyn is a creative and professional writer with 13+ years of experience in marketing, advertising and business communications. She's a mother, a lover of good food and painting rooms, and a writer of science fiction, paranormal fantasy, and more. You can find more of Kaitlyn's work at kpetrywrites.ca.

The Librarian's Tale

It happened subtly at first.

Destiny Roberts, BA, BEd, MLS, newly qualified librarian, entered the library of Canterbury High on the first day of the new school year ready to welcome students.

It was her first library contract, and she'd spent the week before decorating the library.

The first odd thing she noticed was that the stapler was not where she'd left it, on the blue tray with all the other office supplies students were allowed to use without asking for permission. She was sure it'd been there when she'd left after setting up on Friday, but perhaps a member of the staff had come into the library on the weekend? She set the stapler back on the blue tray and turned on the overhead lights.

The second odd thing happened that afternoon when she walked into the storage room and found a large envelope full of a Shakespeare themed bulletin board kit on the floor. It hadn't been there earlier. She knew no one had been in this storage room, since she was the only person with a key to the room, aside from the custodian who wasn't on duty yet.

There were lots of envelopes full of posters and letters for assorted bulletin board displays in the filing cabinet. She'd flipped through them last week when she was checking on the supplies in her new library. She hadn't noticed this particular envelope, but it had to have come from the cabinet. It was too thick for someone to have pushed it under the door. She filed it back in the cabinet, picked up the DVD player Mrs. Marshall the chemistry teacher had signed out, and locked the door behind her.

The third odd thing happened the next morning. When she walked into the library, she saw that her lovely 'Welcome to the Library ~ Have a great year!' bulletin board display had been transformed into a promotional bulletin board for the Globe Theatre with "Shakespeare's Advice" highlighting the quotation, "We are such stuff as dreams are made on and our little life is rounded with a sleep."

Destiny recognized the quotation from *The Tempest*. She wondered if someone was playing a practical joke on her.

It wasn't that she disliked Shakespeare. She'd done an English degree before her education credentials and a Masters in Library Sciences, but there was a time and a place. The first week of school, it was time for a welcome message in the library, not a Shakespeare lesson.

She went back to her desk to get the staple remover.

Just as she was reaching for it, there was a crash: something had fallen on the far side of the library. She ran to look and found a whole row of books from the 540s on the floor. Did some student have a vendetta against chemistry?

"This isn't funny!" she called out.

There was no response. She tiptoed through the end of the stacks, checking each row, but she was the only person in the library. She tightened her lips, glared at the Shakespeare bulletin board, and returned to the circulation desk to turn on the computer. The first bus of students would be arriving any moment.

At noon, an email message popped up that Ms. Roberts had a parcel in the school office.

When she pushed through the office door, Mrs. Boisvert looked up from her desk. "Uh oh. That's a scary face. What's going on?"

"Is there anyone besides me who has a key to the library?"

Mrs. Boisvert was keeper of the keys. She shook her head. "The custodial staff have all access C keys," she said, "and Dr. Scott, of course. That's it. You're the only one issued the L key. Why?"

"Because someone is sneaking into the library and moving stuff around. Yesterday it was objects. Today there's an entire bulletin board display that I didn't make."

"That's weird."

"Yeah. Instead of a welcome display, I've got a Shakespeare display. Can you think of anyone who'd play a prank like that?"

Mrs. Boisvert could. For decades there'd been someone at Canterbury High who would have delighted in such a prank, but he was gone now. She shook her head. "No one has time for things like that the first week of school."

"That's what I thought." Ms. Roberts picked up the box of new books. "If you hear anything, would you let me know?"

"Of course, dear," said Mrs. Boisvert, standing so she could open the office door for Mrs. Roberts. "I'm sure it's very unsettling for you."

"It is freaking me out, to be honest. I guess people always like to play tricks on the new staff member, so they can figure out whether they're a good sport."

"I suppose that's a possible reason," said Mrs. Boisvert, watching Ms. Roberts as she headed down the hall. Mrs. Boisvert returned to her desk muttering, "I don't like the look of this."

"What's don't you like?" asked Dr. Scott emerging from the staff room.

"I think," said Mrs. Boisvert, settling behind her computer again, "we have a something strange going on at Canterbury."

"Oh?," Dr. Scott chortled, then he noticed her expression. "Stranger than usual?"

"Maybe..." said Mrs. Boisvert. But right then, the fire alarm starting blaring.

"Oh shit," said Dr. Scott, heading to the hallway. "I wonder who's pulled that now?"

Mrs. Boisvert picked up her emergency procedures clipboard and followed him murmuring, "I have an idea" to herself.

oooooo

Mrs. Roberts was kept busy over the next couple of days cataloguing the new books, so it was Friday before she went looking for the stapler remover to deal with the bulletin board. She hunted through every desk drawer, but the fancy straight staple remover was gone. Nor could she find the pincer one that had been in the circulation desk. The one that had been attached to the office stapler was gone, too. "This is ridiculous," she muttered, wondering if she could just sneak a knife out of the staff room kitchen.

That's when she glanced up and noticed a series of stars

had been added to the bulletin board ad that the "Shakespeare's Advice" quote had changed. Now she was being advised, "Stars hide your fires. Let not light see my black and deep desires."

"Well, that's ominous," she muttered. "Is that from *Macbeth*? It must be. Who else had black and deep desires?"

"Excuse me?" said a student in volleyball uniform, dropping a book in the return bin. "Did you say something to me?"

"No dear," said Destiny Roberts, hoping she wasn't blushing. "Just talking to myself."

"Ah," said the girl, as she hustled out of the room.

"Great," said Destiny and then looked around to see if any more students would think she was crazy. Her eyes settled once more on the bulletin board.

Why would anyone spend so much time trying to play a prank on her? She wasn't going to be threatened by someone's weird sense of humour. This was just silly. She would pull the display off with her bare hands.

She approached the display, lunch knife in hand, determined to remove it.

There was a thump behind her, then another one. She whirled around to see books leaping one by one off the 797s shelf, like a row of synchronized swimmers entering a pool. "What the hell?" She looked around the room for whoever was doing this. "Come on! You're just making more work for me!" She arrived at the shelf just as the last book went over the edge. She grabbed it mid-air and turned it around, examining it for wires or magnets. There were none. She studied the shelf. She couldn't see anything out of the ordinary. No hidden mechanisms to propel books. But books don't just leap off shelves.

She looked back at Shakespeare bulletin board and then down at the knife still in her hand. Behind her, another book thudded to the floor. "All right!" she said to the empty room. "Fine! You win! I'll leave it up!"

She stomped back to her desk. Only one week at Canterbury High and it was not turning out to be the respectful and considerate place Dr. Scott had made it out to be when he hired her. She didn't like this one bit.

On Monday, the quote on the board said, "So wise so young, they say, never do live long." She had to look that one up. It was from *Richard the Third*.

On Tuesday, the board declared, "And so from hour to hour we ripe and wrought and then from hour to hour we brought and bought and thereby hangs a tail." Her search said that one came from *As You Like It*.

On Wednesday, it said, "If you prick us, do we not bleed? If you tickle us, do we not laugh? If you poison us, do we not die? And if you WRONG US, shall we not REVENGE?"

Destiny Roberts didn't like the capitals on that quote from *The Merchant of Venice*. A new teacher prank was one thing, but someone threatening her wasn't a prank: it was workplace harrassment. She didn't need that kind of crap.

Thursday when she looked at the quote on the wall it read, "So wise, so young they say, ne'er do live long."

"Huh," she said, "That's kind of depressing for a high school."

"What is?"

"Destiny whirled around to see a smiling and elegant woman. "Sorry, I didn't hear you come in. I was miles away."

"Je m'excuse," the woman laughed, in a throaty French accent. "I'm Génèvieve Marchand, the French teacher. You were looking at the board?"

"Yes. A new quote has appeared every day. Yesterday it was threats. Today's is a bit fatalistic." She waved her arm toward the board.

"Ahh," Mme. Marchand nodded, "I see what you mean. But wisdom is not in great supply around here, so I'm sure we will all live forever."

Destiny laughed and turned away from the board. "I will ignore it until the next quote appears."

"Why not change it now if you don't like it?"

"I can't. Weird things happen when I try." She shrugged. "I've given up."

"Someone is playing a trick on you, surely?" Mme. Marchand reached toward the quote, slipping her nail under a staple, and a crash sounded on the other side of the room. She jumped in surprise, snapping her hand back.

"Here we go again," sighed Destiny, looking down the stacks for the fallen books. This time it was the 914 section. "This is a coincidence," said Destiny, picking up a lovely colour anthology of French historical sites and tilting the cover toward Génèvieve. "France."

Génèvieve took the book and studied the cover. "Not just France. This picture is from my home village." A shiver ran up her spine as she set the book on the shelf. She looked over to the Shakespeare display. "Did you say it just appeared?"

"Yes. And any time I try to touch it, books fly around. It's quite the practical joke."

Génèvieve bit her lip. "Oui," she said.

"Was there something you were looking for?" said Destiny.

"I signed my class up for computers and research. I just thought I'd come say hello while I was here. I'm sorry to have startled you."

"It's okay. I'm finding myself startled on a regular basis in this library. It's a weird place."

"C'est vrai," muttered Génèvieve as she gave a little wave to Destiny.

She walked right down the hall, through the office and

rapped on the principal's door. Dr. Scott was sitting at his desk staring at his computer screen. "Come," he called.

She opened the door. "Dr. Scott," she said, "I need to talk to you."

Dr. Scott unfolded his huge frame from his chair and smiled welcomingly. "Of course, Génèvieve. What can I do for you?"

"You can get a ghost out the library," she said as she stared at him with an expression that did not brook any nonsense. "Destiny Roberts is being haunted. He needs to go. You're in charge. You need to deal with it."

"Ah," he said, leaning over to look through his door into the outer office. "Mrs. Boisvert, can you join us, please?"

Dr. Scott settled himself back into his chair and the women sat on the other side of the desk. "Mrs. Boisvert, Génèvieve believes we have a ghost in the library."

Mrs. Boisvert nodded complacently, as if this were the kind of news routinely brought into her office.

"I'm not joking," said Génèvieve. "That ass has stayed behind to haunt us! He's wreaking havoc in the library! Poor Destiny has a haunted bulletin board that he updates with creepy messages. When she touches it, he has a tantrum and throws books around!"

"Ms. Roberts has not mentioned anything about creepy messages or flying books," said Dr. Scott, rubbing his chin.

"Of course, she hasn't." Génèvieve rolled her eyes. "She's a first year teacher. She doesn't want you to think she's whacko."

"She doesn't strike me as the whacko type," said Mrs. Boisvert to Dr. Scott with a shrug, "but then again, you never can tell what comes out in the wash."

"Merci, Madame," glowered Génèvieve. "Can you think of anyone who loved being at this school enough that if he died, he'd want to stay and haunt it?" she asked, one eyebrow raised.

"Sure, Mr…" Dr. Scott stopped before he said the name and stared at her. "He couldn't."

Génèvieve tilted head toward Mrs. Boisvert.

Mrs. Boisvert nodded, "He would."

"But there are no such thing as ghosts," Dr. Scott whispered.

"Let's hope there's not," sighed Mrs. Boisvert, "because there are a few people around here that he's probably angry with."

"Oui," Génèvieve gave a little shiver. "Like *moi*."

Mrs. Boisvert leaned back in her chair. "I don't think there's a department in the building upon which he wouldn't want to exact revenge.

Dr. Scott shivered as he walked into his office. "A vengeful ghost. God, I hope not. I thought we were finally rid of him and could have a peaceful school year at last."

Destiny arrived at Canterbury an hour before the start of classes and flipped on the lights in the library. She took four steps into the room and all the lights turned off. She whirled around, "Hey!"

There was no one there.

A shiver tingled along her spine. She swallowed, trying to moisten a suddenly dry mouth. There was an odd scent in the air, some bargain store cologne of the kind marketed to pubescent boys with the promise it will make them irresistable to girls. Gross. She walked back and flipped the lights on again, then strode purposely into the library office. She felt a finger track along the back of her neck.

She tipped her shoulder so her book bag dropped down to her palms. She grabbed the handle and swung to knock out whoever was behind her.

Her momentum swung her in a circle and she fell

backwards against the desk.

There was a low chortle.

"This isn't funny!" she shouted.

Papers on her desk fanned out.

Destiny's heart began to pound harder.

Her computer screen blinked on.

She watched in horror as the keys on her keyboard depressed, entering a password.

Her password?

A blank document opened up.

Why do we study Shakespeare? appeared across the page.

"Are you asking me?" she squeaked.

The typing continued with bullet points:

* to learn about betrayal
* to learn how to exact vengeance

"You know," said Destiny, "Hamlet's ghost didn't do so well. Remember Polonius? Perhaps you'd be better off just heading to whatever afterlife you were supposed to get to."

"Though those that are betray'd do feel the treason sharply, yet the traitor stands in worse case of woe." appeared on the screen.

More threatening Shakespeare. "Look," said Destiny, "I'm new here. I don't know what your problem is. Why are you haunting my library?" She realized as she spoke that she sounded rather whiny, but if ever there was a reason to whine, surely it had to be having a grumpy ghost colleague at work? "Can you tell me what's happened? Why are you still here?"

Across the screen in bold letters appeared "Machinations, hollowness, treachery, and all ruinous disorders, follow us disquietly to our graves."

Destiny Roberts put her hand across her mouth to hold back the scream that threatened. She could feel her head swimming. "Surely not?" she whispered.

"Some villain hath done me wrong."

"Who killed you?" Destiny asked the screen.

Upon the screen appeared, "we Caesar's friends, that have abridged his time of fearing death. Stoop, Romans, stoop, and let us bathe our hands in Caesar's blood."

"Your friends killed you? Do you want me to do something about it?"

There was a rush of wind and all the papers on her desk rose is a swirling whirlwind then tumbled to the floor where they clearly spelled out, "Y E S."

Destiny took a quivering breath. "All right, then. I'll see what I can do. I'm not a detective though, you understand. I'm not making any promises. Is that good enough for you?

The papers on the floor swirled up in another whirlwind and arranged themselves back into a tidy pile on the desk. She nodded once. "Excuse me," she announced to the empty room. "I think I need a coffee."

oooooo

She left the library doors unlocked, as she crossed to the staff room. She was standing quivering beside the coffee maker when Dr. Scott came in.

"Ah. Ms. Roberts. I've been meaning to speak to you."

"Oh?" she said, attempting a nonchalant sip of her coffee. Her hand shook so much, there were waves in her cup.

"Is everything all right?"

She nodded. "I'm fine thanks." She attempted another sip of her coffee. It sloshed onto the floor. She burst into tears.

"Here," said Dr. Scott, reaching for her cup. "Let me take that." He had to pry her fingers off the handle. "Why don't you have a seat?" He nodded to the old leather couch.

Destiny dropped onto the couch and buried her face in her hands.

Dr. Scott pulled up one of the smaller chairs around the

long table and set it across from Destiny. "Can you tell me what's wrong?"

She shook her head.

"Is it a student?" he asked, with a hopeful tone.

She shook her head.

"A staff member?" He noticed the box of tissue on the table and handed her the box.

Destiny wiped her eyes with the back of her hand. "Everyone has been lovely. Just lovely."

She pulled a tissue and dabbed at her red eyes, blinking quickly.

He gave a little cough. "It wouldn't, by any chance, be a ghost?"

Destiny stared at him, then nodded mutely. Then she whimpered and covered her eyes with her arm.

"Damn," said Dr. Scott. "I was really hoping they were wrong about that."

Destiny wiped her eyes and murmured, "At the interview, you didn't say you had a haunted school."

"I didn't know I did. It seems to be a new thing." He rubbed his bald head and closed his eyes. "Has the ghost said anything?"

Destiny sniffed. "It seems to think it's been betrayed and murdered."

"Hmm."

"It seems," she sniffed, "interested in vengence."

"Well, he would, I imagine," Scott murmured.

"Pardon me? Do you know who the ghost is?"

"If I had to guess, I'd say it was our English department head who died last year. But I assure you, he died of natural causes. He had a stroke at his desk. The autopsy identified it."

"That doesn't seem a reason to become a ghost. What's there to revenge? What would have upset him?"

"Well, when he didn't show up at the end of the year, everyone just presumed he'd taken off to avoid the fuss of the retirement party. It turned out he'd set up a secret office in a room that had been officially sealed." He paused for a moment before adding, "The pathologist's best guess was that he'd died in June, likely the day the report cards were due, since the reporting program was up on his computer."

Destiny's nostrils flared as she considered the ramifications of that. "Oh dear."

"Yeah. Exactly." Dr. Scott shifted as the quiver ran up his spine. "We found his body the end of August, when we were starting the new school year. It wasn't pleasant."

"You mean last month?"

Mrs. Boisvert the secretary came into the room and glanced at Destiny before filling her coffee cup.

"No, no," said Dr. Scott. This was last year. He had plenty of time to haunt the school last year and he didn't. I don't know why he'd show up a year later to cause trouble."

"I'll bet it was because there weren't any new female teachers last year," Mrs. Boisvert said, sipping her coffee and taking a seat at the table. "I can't see him wanting to haunt Mr. Warren or Mr. Davies." The two young men had been the only hires last year.

Destiny rolled her eyes, "Are you suggesting this is his way of ghostly flirting with me?"

"It's not so unreasonable for him," murmured Dr. Scott.

"There's nothing reasonable about a ghost." Destiny scowled at them. "Do we believe in ghosts? Honestly? Surely this just has to be some cruel practical joke by one of the students. Is there someone in the physics club who could pull a prank like this?"

Mrs. Boisvert and Dr. Scott exchanged chagrined glances. Finally, Mrs. Boisvert met Destiny's eyes. Mr. Thompson's old classes might have been able to come up with some sort of prank, but the ones who knew Mr. Edwards have all graduated now. Besides, you've looked for strings, magnets, and whatnot, haven't you?"

Destiny nodded. "I did. I cleared shelves and studied all the books that leapt off them. I didn't find a thing."

Génèvieve Marchand walked in and headed to the coffee pot.

Mrs. Boisvert closed her eyes and sighed. "As ridiculous as it sounds, Mr. Edwards was definitely the kind of man who would return to school to haunt a new, young, female teacher. Moreover, you're precisely the type of woman upon whom he most commonly preyed."

"Preyed upon?" Destiny squeaked. "You had some kind of lecher on staff?"

Dr. Scott cleared his throat, "I'm afraid the magnitude of his actions didn't become clear until after his death. Quite a few people had experienced, shall we say, unwelcome attention and irritation over the years, but it wasn't until staff were discussing things openly that administration realized he should have been reprimanded years ago." He looked at Mme. Marchand. "I do apologize I didn't see the breadth of the distress he was causing you, for example."

Génèvieve shrugged, "It's done now. You can't help the awkwardness that ensues in a workplace after consentual relationships end badly. I chose to believe he was *romantique*." She shrugged and added, "As it turned out, I made a bad choice."

Dr. Scott nodded sympathetically.

Mrs. Boisvert said, "So, what are we going to do about him now? We can't have him haunting Destiny's library, messing her displays and tossing around the books."

"Halloween is coming." Dr. Scott said. "It wouldn't look

weird if everyone dressed up for a Halloween staff party in the library."

"Are you suggesting a séance?" Génèvieve laughed, "Remember how Norton hated staff socials."

Dr. Scott "He'll hate this one, even more than most. Never mind a séance. If it's Norton Edwards, we know why he's here. I'll find an exorcist. We'll get him out of the building for good."

Mrs. Boisvert nodded. "That could work."

Mme. Marchand smirked. "Bon ideé."

Ms. Destiny Roberts inhaled deeply. "I guess it's worth a try."

They looked at him expectantly and Dr. Scott coughed again. "Um. Mrs. Boisvert, do you have any idea where I can find an exorcist?"

Mrs. Boisvert stood up, and smoothed down her brown tweed skirt. "I'll see what I can find," she said, and headed into the main office. The staff room door clicked shut behind her.

Mme. Marchand patted her hand over Destiny's. "It will be okay. Once Mme. Boisvert is on the case, the problem is always solved."

"Hey," said Dr. Scott. "I solve problems!"

"Oui, oui," said Génèvieve. "Of course you do." She winked at Destiny.

The following week, on October 30th, quite a large group of staff members appeared in the library. There were no practices, games, or extra-curricular activities scheduled after school, so there were no students. Mrs. Bell, the custodian, locked the school doors and left a note with her cell phone in case someone needed in urgently.

A few staff members had seen three men in clerical collars enter the building just before the end of the school day. The trio had gone immediately into Dr. Scott's office. After the building had been emptied, Dr. Scott took them to what had been Mr.

Edwards's secret office.

They hadn't stayed long. "He's definitely not here," Génèvieve overhead one say in the hall. "Where have the hauntings been?"

Dr. Scott took him to the library. The man had nodded. "Gather the participants here. I will start in an hour."

The library overhead lights were off, leaving only the small lamps on the study tables. All the staff who'd known Mr. Edwards were there.

"Where did Dr. Scott find an exorcist?" asked Chris Toffler, the art teacher to Karen Mac, the chemistry teacher.

"Mrs. Boisvert, I believe."

"Ah. That woman is a marvel. Whatever will we do when she retires?"

"Let's hope she decides to return as a ghost and keeps running the office, or the place will completely fall to pieces."

Behind them there was a cough. They turned to find Mrs. Boisvert looking at them. "I assure you," she said, "I will have better things to do when I retire."

At that moment, a stout man in very ornate clerical vestments, including a conical hat and a long golden staff with a curl at the top, entered the library. All chatter stopped. Behind him walked two other strangers, also in ornate vestments.

"*Ecce crucis signum, fugiant phantasmata cuncta,*" said the stout man. The heavy scent of sage filled the room as one man swung a smoking brass thurible back and forth. Behind him another robed man sprinkled water to either side with an aspergillum. They circled the room while the most ornately dressed one continued to intone in Latin. Génèvieve thought probably Norton was the only one on staff who might have understood it.

Dr. Scott walked behind the trio.

"He looks rather sheepish, don't you think?" whispered Mr.

Toffler to Ms Mac.

"Wouldn't you?" Ms. Mac snickered.

Destiny glared at them and they looked contritely down at their feet.

"*Ecce crucis signum, fugiant phantasmata cuncta*" intoned the bishop as the trio rounded the far corner and came toward the assembled teachers.

Mme. Marchand crossed herself and watched as the trio processed past everyone and left the library.

The staff looked at each other.

That's it? Mr. Toffler mouthed to Mme. Marchand, who shrugged in reply.

Dr. Scott cleared his throat. "I believe that is the end of exorcism." He bit his lip. "Thank you for coming." He raised his eyebrows, sucked air through gritted teeth and added plaintively, "Please don't mention this to anyone outside the building?"

The staff nodded soberly, as they rose slowly to their feet and ambled out of the library in twos and threes. Most were silent. A few murmured and looked between the Shakespeare display and Destiny.

"Bonne chance," said Mme. Marchand, setting her hand on Destiny's shoulder. "Let's hope."

Destiny nodded.

Mrs. Boisvert walked past. "I have a good feeling about this," she said.

"Was Mr. Edwards even Catholic?"

Mrs. Boisvert laughed. "No. Church of England. He did love a good spectacle, though. Have you thought of a way to test that this worked?"

Destiny nodded her chin toward the Shakespeare bulletin board. "I changed the message this afternoon."

The board read, "Forever and forever farewell, Edwards. If

we do meet again, we'll smile indeed. If not, t'is true this parting was well made."

"Shakespeare had a character called Edwards?"

"Well no." Destiny smiled. The phrase occurs twice in *Julius Caesar*, once by Cassius and once by Brutus. They name each other. But I figured the message would be unequivocal this way."

Dr. Scott joined them as Destiny rose. "I saw the bulletin board. Let's hope all this worked."

They turned off lamps and the women exited the room. Dr. Scott paused at the threshold and spoke loudly, "The pathologist said you had a stroke, Norton. Nothing to do with anyone here. Let it be. Move on." He shut the door firmly and crossed his fingers.

The next morning, Destiny Roberts unlocked the door to her library. A faint wisp of sage hung in the air. She looked on the bulletin board and her heart filled her throat.

All the words had fallen off the board but two:

Farewell.

Edwards.

"All right," she said to the empty room. "Let's find something upbeat for this bulletin board."

SHAWN L. BIRD

Shawn L. Bird is an author, poet, and educator in the stunning Shuswap region of British Columbia. Author of over thirty publications, her 2018 novella *Murdering Mr. Edwards* was nominated for the Lou Allin Memorial Best Crime Novella prize of the Arthur Ellis Awards for excellence in Canadian Crimewriting.

MARIE POWELL

Angel Wing

The accordion keeps time with the tap of our shoes on the hardwood floor of the church basement. It's a polka, like the one they played that night, at Cousin Doreen's wedding. Anne looks pleased when I choose her as my partner. She barely comes up to my shoulder, lean and strong, the easiest woman to lead. A gaggle of her friends watch us from the sidelines as we glide into the turn. Then I'm gone. And she's alone in the swirl of dancers and staring women.

I wait by the Angel Wing plant in the corner of her living room. My sister huddles under the wool blanket on the couch, where insomnia drives her at night. I rustle the Angel Wing's leaves. She yelps awake. Struggles out of the blanket, stands, and folds it ready for tomorrow. I try rustling the leaves again, but she turns away and walks to the window.

It's not really called an Angel Wing, I want to say. An Angel Wing is a begonia. This plant, with its big spotted leaves split into two hearts, is a caladium. An Elephant Ear. She cared for this plant for two months before I told her that. I wonder if she remembers.

"Anne." Gord stomps in, carrying a toolbox in his good

hand. He never knocks.

"Ah," she says, as if startled.

He mumbles an excuse, then nods at the Angel Wing. He can't see me. I'm pretty sure of that. But he nods. Then he raises the toolbox.

"Taps in the main bathroom," she says.

"Shower head too?" He frowns.

"Don't think so. Just the taps."

He nods, gesturing toward the window. "Foggy, this morning."

She moves to the vertical blinds, as if she's still dancing. The blinds creak apart, and she stares out the window at the fog. It hangs heavy across the acreage, like an ocean has crept in overnight, hiding the valley. The shed is invisible. I know it's there. Of course, it's there.

"Blood red moon again last night." Her voice is almost a whisper.

Gord doesn't answer right away. He could tell her the colour of the moon is caused by particles in the atmosphere, from forest fires up north drifting down to us. He could say the fog is condensation in the air, caused by the weather changing.

"It's August," he says.

"Wait five minutes." Standard response. *Don't like the weather in Saskatchewan? Wait five minutes. It'll change.* My sister raises her eyebrows and turns from the window toward the coffee maker on the sideboard. First thing she does in the morning is put the coffee on. Last thing she does every night is get it ready. Everything goes better over a cuppa joe, as Dad used to say.

Gord clears his throat. "She here?" The question hangs in the air between us. "Megan, I mean. Saw her in the coffee shop yesterday."

"You had coffee with her?"

"She was all by herself." He shrugs. "She looks like you. You—and Len."

Her mouth is a long, thin line. She pours Gord a cup, not waiting for the pot to fill, putting her own cup under to catch the drips.

"So," he says, as he takes it.

"You know your way around." She turns away. "I got a farm to run."

She heads out through the screen door into the fog. I worry for a minute. She'll have to jiggle the shed door in the moist air. The shed will smell of old dirt and forgotten husks, the way it always does. I wonder if she still keeps vehicles in it.

I know this farm as well as she does. The shed leads into the store on one side, then the greenhouses. Fields beyond that. With fall coming, she'll have a good sprout started in the greenhouses already. Cucumbers, yellow squash, zucchini, and red bell peppers lined up side-by-side on the old table, ready for canning.

Gord's swearing filters through the walls of the house, punctuating the tap and clang of his tools. Twice, water sputters into the sink to clear air from the pipes. Coffee's burned black by the time he sets his toolbox by the door.

"Huh," he says, more to himself than me. He starts a new batch, clearing the cups and clutter into the kitchen as he waits for it to brew. The pot hisses when he pours himself another cup.

The rumble and crunch of a car pulling into the driveway draws me back to the window. Gord shuffles up behind me, wipes his hands on a cloth, and puts it into his back pocket again. The fog is still thick enough that I can't see it, but I hear the car door open and shut.

"Good morning." I hear Anne's voice as she calls out. Voices strain through the haze. Then footsteps as two figures materialize out of the fog, one in a skirt and two-inch heels. All dressed up. That one stumbles on the gravel as Anne leads her toward the house.

"Megan," Gord says, opening the door. As if I wouldn't recognize her anywhere. She shakes his outstretched hand. "You drove here through this?"

"It wasn't that bad."

"I could've brought you. How's Nell?"

She must be staying at Nell's Cottage, the B&B in town. Not here. Anne frowns at the Angel Wing, but I'm not there.

"Did you get my letter?" Megan drifts closer to Anne, maybe for a hug.

"You're welcome here, you know," Anne says.

Gord smiles. "There now."

"You didn't write back. Mom said you didn't call?" Megan says it as a question, not an accusation. It catches me off guard, the softness of her voice. Her eyes, as grey as mine.

"This was his house, too." Anne tries to look away. "Your Dad." And then I'm right behind her, my breath on her ear, my hand raising hers to Megan's hair. *Soft, red hair. Like yours. Like mine.*

"That isn't what I meant." Megan steps back. "Not at all."

I drop my hand, and Anne's falls with it.

"Too bad about the fog," Gord puts in. "You can't see anything out there today. Otherwise, we could give you the grand tour." I glance at him.

"I'd love to see it," Megan says. "What about the greenhouses? Or the house?" She hesitates a bit now. "Dad's room. Might be my only chance to see it."

She can't wait to get away from here. I'm at the Angel Wing again. Leaves rustling.

"Oh, no," Gord says. "You should stay. Here."

"I really need to get back to Regina."

"In this fog? At least stay for lunch. Your aunt's some cook."

Anne checks her watch. "Gord's right. I should start lunch." She turns toward the kitchen.

"Let me help," Megan says, slinging her black shoulder bag over the arm of a chair.

"No need."

"I want to. See the kitchen."

I hear the fridge door open and shut. The slight hiss as Anne turns on the gas stove, the clink of a pot on the burner, the rush in Megan's voice.

"I saw some of the acreage on the Internet. The website looks pretty good."

"Gord did that."

"Really? It's great. The field looks huge."

I want to ask what it's like to see something you've never seen before and know it's yours.

A snap and click as the greens fall into Anne's big wooden serving bowl. She's grating in some carrot. *Thk-thk-thk.* Chopping onion or zucchini? The fridge creaks open again. Probably taking out the bag of antipasto vegetables she cut yesterday.

Gord chatters about the website. It was his winter project. He built one for himself and then made a page for Anne. Phone's been ringing off the hook at his place.

Wooden bowls clatter on the tabletop. Salad first, then soup to follow. I don't need to be in the room to see it in front of them. Bread and cheese, no doubt. Gord will dish out, handing a bowl to Megan first. He'll favor his hand. It's an old injury. Megan will pretend not to notice.

"This is great. How do you make the dressing?"

"Kraft." Anne's voice is light, as if she's making a joke.

"What?"

"Kraft makes it. This is just an old vinegar bottle."

"Oh."

"I suppose you've been visiting your Dad's—old haunts."

"So you did get the letter. What was he—"

"Have you been to the bar yet?" Anne's voice has gone tight, almost bitter.

"You mean the one in town? No, I haven't."

The silence stretches from the kitchen into the living room. To hear her tell it, I went from the table to the truck to the bar to the couch. Sometimes I barely made it to the couch. While she kept everything going.

"We should all go," Gord tries. "Tonight. There's a live band, I think." He crunches on some greens.

"I plan on going back to Regina this afternoon." Megan's breath catches. "I've got my stuff in the car, and I want to get settled in the residence. Unpack. Get my books. All that."

"University," Gord says. "That's right. Your Dad went to university, too. He came up with the idea of going organic after that, didn't he?"

"Native plants," Anne says. "Native to the prairies. Dock, chicory, sorrel, what they call Jerusalem artichoke. We specialize."

"Really?"

Maybe no one's ever told her.

"Ground cover in the spring. Plants and shrubs for landscaping." Anne says it like an offer. "These days, it's more peppers, pumpkins, squash, that kind of thing. Sells well, this time of year."

"Horticulture." Gord almost sings it. "He took horticulture, your dad. In Calgary. That's where he met your mother. Did she tell you that?" There's a pause, and I imagine Megan nods. "Is that what you're taking? Horticulture?"

"No, I'm in Arts."

"An artist? That's great. Do you paint?"

"No. Not an artist. Liberal Arts."

"Oh. Because—"

"I'm not sure what I want to major in yet. Mom says to take some classes, see what sticks."

"An expensive proposition, these days," Gord comments.

"She can afford it," Anne says. She's thinking about the automatic deposit we make to Megan's trust account every month. Whether the farm makes enough money or not.

"Mom invested well."

"A farm's a good investment." Anne voice has a touch of something else now. Fear?

"You can take anything you want, of course." Megan's voice is quiet, but firm. "What's here is as much yours as—"

"Yes, it is."

One chair leg scrapes across the floor, then another. Plates and silverware clink. Water runs into the sink, and the plates whoosh under.

"Leave them."

"All right." The washcloth swishes. Gord's washing up.

Megan's cheeks are flushed as she follows Anne back into the living room. Anne picks up the spritzer and moves toward the Angel Wing. I back up a little.

"It's beautiful." Megan walks toward us. "Huge. Is it a—native plant?"

"No," she says. "They call this an Elephant Ear. Your Dad called it an Angel Wing. He bought it for your mother."

I barely notice she remembers the names. I'm walking behind Megan now, unable to stop myself, whispering.

Joanne always said she couldn't get a plant to grow. Two black thumbs. It was a joke between us. We needed an angel then. So I bought her this plant and took it over to the house. You were at school. I wanted to surprise her. Maybe she'd be so pleased she'd let me in. You never know. She was in her bathrobe. Prettiest woman I've ever known, your mother. Prettiest I've ever seen her, that day. She answered the door. Didn't ask me in. Then I saw him. He walked up behind her. Wearing a towel.

Anne has stopped spritzing now. She's watching us. I move to the window, stare out at the fog.

"My dad?"

"What? Oh, yes. He—he bought it for your mother."

"I've never seen it before."

"He never gave it to her."

Megan says nothing, but she's not surprised. Makes me wonder what she knows. What she's been told.

"He said it was the kind of plant anyone could grow."

"She's not that good with plants."

"So he says. Said. Kept it with him in the shed. I brought it in here. After."

Megan comes closer to the plant. "People say. Things." Her fingers trace the edges of the leaves as if fascinated with their shape. "Mom thinks you can see him." Her voice drops to a whisper. "Is he here, now?"

Anne plucks a few browning leaves with her free hand. She sets them into the plant pot and looks over at me.

"I still see Helen. Sometimes." Gord comes in from the kitchen, finally, and refills his cup at the sideboard. "We were married for thirty years. I turn around and she's standing there. In the kitchen, over by the stove. In her chair in the living room, at night. Reading. Her bare foot brushing mine, in bed."

Anne walks over to the side counter, takes out a photograph album, and sets it down on the coffee table. Megan sits on the couch and opens the cover. Anne points at a photo.

"That's Gord and your Dad. They were best friends. Inseparable. Them and that dog. Your Dad's border collie."

"Laddie," Gord puts in. He gestures with his cup. "Pour you

some?"

"Oh, I can get it," Megan says.

Gord moves closer and flips the album pages. "Don't mind me. Mangled this hand in the thresher, after Helen died." He flips another page. "This is Helen. Anne and her was best friends. She visited the hospital every day when Helen got the cancer. I'll never forget that."

He turns to his favorite picture: Helen and I, hanging decorations in the gym. "Helen was some beauty, eh, Anne?" The night of senior prom. "That's your dad, Megan. I always thought he'd stay here."

Anne says nothing but glances over at me.

"Anne was headed out. Going to Regina to be an artist." He glances at my sister. "She was some painter."

"He's being polite. That was a long time ago. I'm surprised you even noticed. Back then, you only had eyes for Helen."

"Oh, that." Gord brushes the comment away, turning back to Megan. "You should have seen her drawings. Look, here— that's her easel. She used to take it out into the field with her."

"You remember that?" Anne's surprise looks genuine.

"Sure. I've still got one of your paintings, hanging in my living room."

"Did you study art?" Megan asks.

"Had to run this place."

"Her mom and dad—your grandma and grandpa—died in a car accident a few days before graduation. Anne took over here."

"It was supposed to be one year."

"That's right." Gord nods, turning to Megan. "You'd have been a baby. Your dad was going to bring you all home again and take over here." He shakes his head.

"That's all water under the bridge now."

"Wasn't that the year they split up?" Gord never knows

when to quit. Anne closes the photo album, ready to put the damn thing back in the cupboard.

"Wait," Megan says. "Please."

"It's all yours, after all." Anne leaves the album and starts for the sideboard. "I could use some joe. You?"

"That's not what I meant." Megan stands up. Her voice is rough. "When I first came here today, I wasn't sure you'd talk to me. But I need to know." She glances in my direction, behind me, before she turns to Anne. "What happened between you and my Dad? The night he died."

"Old wounds," Gord says. No getting away from this, for any of us.

"Dad was here that whole summer," Megan says, staring hard at Anne, arms folded across her chest. "That's what Mom says."

"And how would she know?" Anne bristles. "She had other things to occupy her time."

"You mean Ted? He's been a good father to me."

Anne glances at me and says nothing.

"Are you saying my mother and Ted caused it?"

"I'm not saying anything against Ted." Anne shakes her head. "Or your mom, for that matter. I wrote to her last year. About the finances, and all. No, I'm not saying that. The timing was bad, that's all."

"Because of Grandma and Grandpa, you mean? The accident?"

"Because of that, yes. Your Dad wanted to bring you all home. He showed up here, with that." She gestures at the plant.

Gord scoffs. "He was in the bar, more than he was here." He pours himself another cup and leans on the sideboard. "You needed him here to help."

"Help? I wanted him to take over. I didn't want this place,

truth be told. I wanted out. And then, Len."

"What? Dad, what? What happened that night?"

I open my mouth. Close it again. I've gone over and over it in my own mind. In the end, nothing changes.

"You make mistakes." Gord is staring right at me. "And that's what your Dad did. Made a mistake." He glances down at his mangled hand. "Easy enough to do."

The leaves of the Angel Wing rustle.

"He had a bit too much, you know, so he left," Gord continues. "We were all still dancing. It was a wedding, after all. Your cousin Doreen, wasn't it, Anne? On the way back, something must have happened with the truck. It was an old truck, don't forget. He pulled into that shed. We used to work on the vehicles there, in those days. It was windy that night. Cold for August. He shut the door. That's all. One minute he's working on the truck. The next—" Gord shrugs.

"Mom said he knew better. He'd been working in that shed since he was a kid. She said he knew better than to shut the door."

"Coroner said the wind speed was forty-seven that night," Gord says. Anne starts to speak, but Gord brushes her words away. "You all believed the worst. I tried to tell you, but you didn't want to hear. Coroner called it an accident. He don't say that to make the family feel better. He says it because he's got the science to prove it. The wind would have been whistling right into the shed. Len closed the door to keep out the wind. Two minutes. That's all it took. There was a bird in that shed with him, and it died with its wings spread. In flight. Toolbox was open. Screwdriver in his hand. Two minutes, the coroner said."

"Why did he leave the wedding?" Megan steps past Gord, and stares straight at Anne. "That's what I don't understand."

"Drank the well dry," Gord says.

"You came all this way to ask me that?" Anne says, ignoring Gord. "I've been paying your half. Every month since the day he died. Even when I didn't make enough to pay it."

"You've been paying mom." Her voice was hot with unshed tears. "After dad died, you paid her off. But I want to know. I have a right."

"A right?" Anne spits back. "You have a right to share the bankruptcy with me, if that's what you want."

"What?"

"This farm is bankrupt, that's what. There's no money to share. I've been paying you out of my own savings."

"Why didn't you say something?" Gord cuts in. "We can work that out."

"That's not even what I'm asking," Megan interrupts. "I don't care about any of that. I want to know what happened."

"What did your mom tell you?"

"When I was young, she told me he went away. Later she told me he'd died. The day I turned eighteen, she told me the rest."

"In June?"

"That's right. The week of exams. Lucky I had an exemption in most of them. She told me what she knew. That Dad had made a will naming me his heir. She knew some of the story from what people told her, at the funeral. But there was a lot she didn't know."

"Like what?"

Gord's staring at the Angel Wing. At me. "You were dancing," Gord says. "Before he left the wedding. You were dancing with him, Anne. Helen saw you. Arguing, she thought."

Megan takes a deep breath. "What happened between you and him?"

"Nothing happened. I wanted to sell the farm. Split the money. He didn't. It was an old argument." Anne starts to clean up the cups, but Megan won't let it rest.

"Why would you stay here?"

"Anyone can make a mistake."

"I phoned the Coroner," Gord says. "Helen never mentioned it, after that."

"He kept humming that polka, over and over, all summer," Anne says.

"Sing me back home," Gord sings, "just one more time."

"That's the one." Anne turns to me. "When it came on, he grabbed me and started dancing. I was so mad. He was supposed to help me. He promised. Said he'd help me bring in the field he left me to plant."

In five steps she covers the distance between us, but she doesn't look at me. "The leaves were starting to wither. He promised. And he let me down again. 'Can't you see we're going to lose half the field?' I asked him. 'Can't you see?'"

It'll be fine. You worry too much—

"You agreed to let me sell." Anne glances at Megan. "He agreed. I said, 'I have the papers now, and they're waiting for an answer. It's a good deal, Len. All you have to do is sign it.'"

I'll never let it happen.

"'That money will help both of us,' I told him. 'You can go back to Calgary and win Joanne back.' I begged him. I'd been accepted to the art college in Regina. I needed that money."

Wait one more year. Native plants make sense as ground cover, especially here. The science is sure. I can make Joanne see that, too. Bring her back here. Give me one more year.

"It's hard work to run a farm. You can't just dream about it." Anne turns away from me, like she did on the dance floor years ago. "But that's what he did. He dreamed this farm, and then made me carry the dream." She laughs, a brittle, unpleasant sound.

"He cared," Gord says. "He cared about you and about this

place."

Anne turns to Megan. "He made you his heir, and more than that. This farm can't be sold until you're twenty-one."

"What? How—"

"It's the way he worded his will. He wrote it out by hand. Had it lawyer-ized at some point." Anne picks up the spritzer again. "So it's your turn, now."

"To do what?" Megan asks.

Anne turns to stare at me.

"To live here," Gord suggests.

"Three more years?" Megan makes an impatient gesture with one hand. "I'm a city kid. I don't know the first thing about farming."

"Neither did I, once."

"And you learned," Gord says. "You learned, didn't you? So now you can teach her."

"I didn't know about the will until after." Anne pinches off a dry leaf and sprays the Angel Wing. "After the funeral. That's when I found the will."

Megan suddenly moves, a brisk walk toward the farmhouse door.

"Go ahead, open it," Anne says, and Megan does. Sunshine floods into the room. But she hesitates on the threshold, looking out.

"The door of the shed." Megan's voice is quiet, so quiet I almost don't hear her.

Gord says nothing, for once. I'm standing behind Megan now, looking over her shoulder. The day is rainbow clear. Anne pinches off another withered leaf.

"You know, this plant is so hardy. Like him. Your Dad. I've had it for so long. You should have it now."

MARIE POWELL

Marie Powell's short stories appear in such literary magazines as *Room* and *subterrain*. Her castle-hopping adventures across North Wales led to her medieval fantasy series *Last of the Gifted*: *Spirit Sight* and *Water Sight*, set in 13th Century Wales. Her 40+ children's books are available through Scholastic, Amicus, and others.

HALLI REID

My Dearest Margot

My dearest Margot,

Of all the ills the world can give and every hurt a man can suffer, the worst of agonies befalls me now. That is, the pain of abandonment. The fever, the one that racked my body for days on end, it was a physical bitterness, and yet my soul was unaffected by it. A soul will always have more power than mere flesh. But there are things that can permanently damage a soul, things far worse than illness or injury.

When I finally awoke, I found myself alone in a tight space, restrictive and confining. My elbows locked at my sides. My feet bound together. Breathing was difficult as a shroud covered my face. I called for help. The same call I often made in the throughs of the fever. Oh, how   I called, 'Margot! Please release me from this nightmare!' I thought I would feel your cool hand on my brow or hear your soft singing to sooth me, as was your usual response. But not this time. This time I felt a chill in my bones, the kind that only comes with the realization of a morbid truth. Removed from my death bed, all hope for me lost, I lay beside my parents in the family crypt.

If your distress was so great that you failed to recognize my shallow breath, I do not blame you. If the physician declared loss of life, then I declare him a buffoon. But if by chance it was Peter who pulled you from the room to comfort you in your grief, then I question his part in the whole affair. Did you see him slip money into the hands of the doctor? The mortician? Did he shield your eyes, bring you to his chest, wipe away your tears? If you witnessed any of these actions, take them as evidence of his deception.

It took me many days to free myself from the grip of death. The bindings on my limbs proved extremely difficult, not surprising since I suspect they were intended for a living victim. Breaking the seal of the tomb was awkward and cumbersome from a prone position. Dust filled the cavity and I wasted precious moments waiting for it to settle. All I thought of in those dark hours was returning to you and confronting Peter.

When, finally, I burst forth from my grave, gasping for air and weak from the effort, my eyes beheld the flowers: lilies for everlasting life. My struggle had disturbed them. The vase was smashed, and the petals were broken and strewn on the cobbles. I read your note and have concluded that I cannot appear to you. Not yet. Not in this vulnerable state. I could shatter your heart as I have your bouquet.

I will bide my time collecting evidence against Peter. Once his unlawful act is proven, you will hurry back to the crypt, crying out for your Lorne, and upon seeing the seal broken, your heart will leap from your chest with all hope restored. I cherish the day of our reunion.

With all my love,
Lorne

My dearest Lorne,

I have no words to write but this. The dream of our life together is gone. I am sick with grief. The sun will never shine on me again. I will shut myself away from the world and never come out.

All my love,
Margot

My dearest Margot,

I heard you come in last evening. You came alone and in secret to place new flowers on my tomb. I heard you pick up the broken vase and shed tears while leaning on my headstone. I felt a salty drop seep through a small gap and onto my fingers. I longed to open the lid and hold you in my arms and rescue you from your sorrows. It would be wonderful, if only it wouldn't scare you. Being witness to the rising dead creates the stuff of nightmares.

I feel closer to death now than I did under the spell of sickness. I thought the cold would be a welcome relief after the intense fever that trapped me in an inferno for so long. The shivering alone takes most of my strength. I creak when I walk. I spend the nights wandering back roads, keeping out of sight and scrounging for scraps like a stray dog. The silent bones of my ancestors are only the company I keep. There is nowhere better for me to lay my head. Though I tried a tree, a ditch, a pig sty and even a hay stack, I return to the crypt to get out of the howling wind and off the damp earth.

Having illicitly procured a candle, ink and parchment I lie in my tomb and write letters to you; letters I know I cannot send. Nevertheless, I document my experience hoping one day you will know of the suffering I endured at Peter's hand. So that you will forgive me when I hunt him down and kill him. I have yet to determine the means. If only the mere sight of me would stop his heart, the blame would fall to his weak constitution instead of myself, but I fear violence is the only effective course of action.

He must have fled like a coward because I cannot find him. His mother alone resides at the estate. The old coot has a keen eye and nearly caught me twice in my attempt to raid the chicken coop. She says nothing of her son, at least not that I have overheard. She does talk in her sleep, so I will wait and listen until she involuntarily reveals his whereabouts.

Until then, my love, do not despair. All things will mend themselves shortly.

Yours,
Lorne

P.S.
I express to you my true regret at breaking another vase.

Dearest Lorne,

I know I cannot hide away from the world forever, still I cannot face society just yet. Imagine Sissy and the others forcing a plethora of delicate questions upon me, the answers of which are too heart wrenching to speak aloud. I am griped with turmoil.

Peter has been nothing but cordial since your death. It is as I predicted. He always held himself back out of respect for our relationship and now that the barricade is cleared away, he puts forth great effort to find my favour. He remains as undisciplined as ever; a romping puppy with no direction. He will never be the man you were. He cannot stand in your place, not even in your shadow.

I remain in my grief,
Margot

My Dearest Margot,

I feel my flesh begin to falter. It hangs off me like wasted wax paper from the butcher. It wraps my meat, holds me together, but feels unattached and poorly wrapped. One nudge from gravity and it will slide off completely, a wrinkled, messy heap on the floor. My diminished state cannot recover from the fever, and I waste away still. Whatever I eat does not satiate the hunger. I suffer like never before. I consume the very dirt beneath my feet, trying to fill my stomach with something, anything.

The light of day gives me terrible migraines. All I can do to avoid it is sleep in my tomb. I sleep excessively, sometimes for days, until the hunger drives me to break a shop-front window and nab whatever is close by. Do you wonder when you walk past the broken pane and compare it to the vases that once held your flowers? Do you know the destroyer is one and the same?

If only you would come to me. Since I shattered that second vase, no other has replaced it. The evidence of vandalism must have frightened you away. You probably suspected grave robbers or criminals had disrupted the crypt and chose to avoid the place for your own safety. How horrible the situation must add to your grief. I sorrow to think of you in distress. I spend hours sorting through the shards, setting each piece back in its place. I can restore the beauty once lost. The glass takes on a new sparkle at every mended seam, shaded pink from my bloody fingertips.

Peter calls on you. He dares have the audacity to speak to you. At least now I know his location. My hunting ground is not his house, but your own. Next time he arrives on your doorstep

I will be there to encase him in his own tomb, to make him suffer as I have suffered. He stole you from me and I will take you back. His punishment will be severe.

Yours forever,
Lorne

Lorne,
 I feel like a fool when I think back at what was done to you. How naive I was! Blinded by love, I sat by your bedside for weeks taking care of you, feeding you, smoothing your hair, cooling your brow. Your will to live surpassed all odds. You held on for weeks longer than you should have.
 Love drives me to do silly things, absolutely obnoxious things. Sissy tells me keeping up appearances is one of my strongest traits, but my impatience gets the better of me more often than not. My façade of despair had gone on long enough to completely entangle Peter to me in pity. Once your affects were cleared out, my invitation to permanently express his condolences directed Peter straight to my bed chamber.
 And now look what you've done. All my efforts are wasted. You've gone and smashed in his brains right on my front stoop. We were finally ready to show ourselves in public. As we waited for the carriage, wishing on the evening star, your ghastly face appeared before us. Accusing Peter of adultery and murder sent him into a tizzy. You used his surprise and disgust to your advantage for I believe if he was better prepared you never would have overpowered him. Not in your present, emaciated state. You match the physique of a skeleton. You left a chunky mess that has stained my steps. I will have to have them replaced.
 As for you, when you wake up you will find yourself

back where you belong, this time with a much better seal. Yelling and crying will only deplete your air supply faster. I suspect you will have just enough to light a candle and read this note. Reread it as many times as will allow. I hope my handwriting and signature are the last things you see as the candle flickers and dies.

Yours in life,
Margot

HALLI REID

Halli Reid has short stories and poetry published in "We Shall be Monsters "with Renaissance Press, "Tesseracts" with Edge Science Fiction and Fantasy, "New Spaces" with Lintusen Press and many others. Her genres range from horror and science fiction to fantasy and poetry. She is a creative writing instructor and a structural editor with essentialedits.ca.

LESLIE WIBBERLEY

A North Wind

Nate

The first time I saw Ptitsa, she appeared out of nowhere.

I was on my way home from class in the middle of one bitch of a storm. The rain, that miserable late November crap, half rain, half sleet, was only a degree away from being full-on snow. I drove at a crawl, barely able to see through the rivers of slush sliding down my windshield.

One minute she wasn't anywhere, and the next, *bam*, there she was: standing in the grass at the edge of Johnson Street, across from Henderson Lake.

I swear on my Granny Jo's grave I didn't imagine her.

I blinked, trying to focus on the shape looming in front of me.

The windows had fogged over, so I scrubbed to clear the moisture. When I realized it was a woman, I stomped on the brakes. The car stopped a mere ten feet from where she stood.

Reefing on the door of my rusty, piece of shit car, I yanked it open and jumped out. To my surprise, the woman didn't look up, not even when I slammed the car door. She just stood there, shivering.

The wind blew from the north, driving the rain, heavy with ice crystals, against my skin. It pelted me with tiny, stinging slaps. My sweatshirt and jeans offered little protection. I was as cold as a witch's tit, and could only imagine the state the woman must be in. Her thin, white dress was completely inappropriate for such shitty weather. The dress flapped around her legs like a flag in a windstorm, the wet fabric so sheer her skin tinted the dress pink. As I approached, her chin tipped downwards. A mass of ebony hair swung forward, covering her face.

"Hello?"

No response.

"Hello, Miss. Are you in some sort of trouble?"

Still no reaction. *What the hell, is she deaf?* I walked closer. Gooseflesh littered the bare expanse of skin visible around her neck and shoulders, where her dress, heavy with moisture, had slipped down. I reached out a tentative hand and tapped her on the shoulder. "Can I help you?"

She jerked at my touch, head snapping upright. Hands, pale as moonlight, pushed at the soaking strands of hair hanging across her face. She stared at me.

I stared back, captivated by her unusual appearance.

Her nose was a little too long for her face, her neck thin and elegant like a ballerina's, merging into a narrow and pointed chin. And her cheekbones, they were like sculpted porcelain. She wasn't classically beautiful, her features too sharp for that designation, but striking, for sure.

Her eyes, though, now *they* were beautiful. Huge, ringed with thick, black lashes, they were a deep midnight blue that drew me in and tugged at something inside my chest. My stomach contracted and my breath stuck in my throat, like someone had sucker-punched me.

I couldn't speak.

Time froze. I have no clear memory of how long we stood like that. Unmoving, silent, seemingly oblivious to the cold, we stared at each other in the pounding rain. Then she blinked, and the spell was broken.

My tongue felt thick, swollen, and I stumbled over my words. "Hello. M-My name is... Nate." I extended my hand, not expecting her to take it.

To my surprise, she reached towards me. The sleeve of her dress fell against my forearm, dripping icy wetness across my thin sweatshirt. Her fingertips grazed my hand, her touch so cold it was painful. I stared down at her long, slender fingers and wrapped my own around them. My hand felt huge and hot as an oven. A profound coldness radiated from her fingers. I dropped my hand. The skin burned where her flesh had met mine. I lifted my head in shock. Her indigo gaze captured me once more, driving all thoughts of my burning hand into insignificance.

I found myself stuttering, an odd occurrence for me. I'm sure I sounded like a babbling fool. "Are y-y-you in t-t-trouble? C-c-can I help you?"

A sigh rippled across her body. Put me in mind of wind lifting the surface of a lake. She remained silent for so long, I wasn't sure she was going to answer me. Then her shoulders dropped sharply, and she spoke.

"I am Ptitsa." Her voice was melodic, her words tinged with an accent I couldn't quite place. She wiped at the raindrops trickling down her face and shivered again, wrapping her arms around her body. "I am so cold."

Oh, my God, Nate. You are such a fucking moron. She's frozen half to death and here you are carrying on a conversation with her like it's a sunny day in July.

"God, I'm so sorry, T-tisa." My tongue tangled in her unusual name. "You must be freezing. Let me grab my coat for you. It's in my car."

I turned and jogged back to the car, still idling behind us. I hadn't dared turn the stupid thing off. No guarantees it would have started again. I yanked the door open and leaned into the backseat, grabbing my red and white varsity jacket. I pulled it forward, jumped out of the car, and ran back to where I'd left Ptitsa standing.

Except that she wasn't. Standing there, I mean. She wasn't anywhere.

oooooo

When I met her for the second time, I wasn't even sure she was the same girl. Dressed in brown leather boots, a black hat, black gloves, and a crimson coat that reached to her knees, she looked like every other girl on campus.

Intent on getting to my next class before my ass froze off, my head was down, collar pulled up against the icy breath of the wind blowing from the north. I would have walked right past her standing at the bus stop if she hadn't called out to me.

Three months had passed since our first meeting. If you could call it that, a meeting. After I'd returned from the car to give her my coat and found her gone, I'd searched the lakeside and surrounding streets. I never found her. She'd simply vanished.

I began to think I'd imagined the whole thing, a reasonable assumption considering the state I'd been in. I'd just pulled an all-nighter studying for an English Lit. exam and spent three long, soul-sucking hours writing an essay on the history of monstrous women in literature. The irony of that wouldn't occur to me until much later.

I hadn't eaten anything except a withered granny smith apple salvaged from our perpetually empty fridge. If you added the five cups of disgusting vending machine coffee I'd downed to keep from falling asleep in class, you had the perfect scenario for a hallucination.

Over the past few months, I'd tried to convince myself that's all it had been, and then, here she was again.

I turned at her, "Hello."

At first, I was confused as to why this random girl called out to me. Then I saw her face...and those eyes. I stopped dead. Took a moment for the words in my head to form themselves into something resembling a comprehensible sentence, and a few more before I was able to wrap my tongue and lips around them and speak. "Hello, yourself."

Hello, yourself? Wow, Nate. Could you be any more pathetic?

She inclined her head, lifting a hand to brush away an errant strand of hair. My eyes followed each graceful motion. Mesmerized, my lungs momentarily declined to draw air.

"I'm sorry I was not able to thank you for trying to provide me with assistance when we first met. I was forced to retreat unexpectedly. I beg your apology."

What a strangely formal manner of speaking. Maybe English

wasn't her first language. That would explain the oddness of her phrasing, and that hint of an accent. "Uhmm...no worries. I-I'm just glad you're okay."

A part of my brain, the part not preoccupied with her incredible eyes, questioned, *Nate, you douche. Don't you want to know how the hell she just disappeared like that?*

She continued before I had a chance to act on that thought. "I am sorry if I caused you concern. That was not my intention, Nate." My name rolled from her pale pink lips like a caress. I found myself staring at them, salivating like a starving man.

She moved closer. A waft of vanilla and cinnamon tickled my nose. I inhaled, savoring the sweetness, her magic once more drawing me in. "Would you care to join me for a cup of coffee?" she asked.

I continued to gaze at her lips, transfixed by their perfection. Imagining how they would taste.

She spoke again, "Nate?"

My cheeks flamed and I wondered how long I'd been staring. *What the hell is it with this girl?* "Uhmm, I, ah." The words refused to come.

"I was hoping you might be willing to join me for coffee, so I may repay your kindness." She smiled, the edges of those perfect lips curling up in the corners and parting, revealing gleaming white teeth. Now I stared at her teeth. They seemed—I don't know—different, somehow. I shook my head and closed my eyes for a second, but when I looked again, her mouth was closed.

I spoke, this time managing to spit out a few intelligible words. "Coffee sounds great, but ah, I'm sorry. I-I have class." I glanced at my watch; I had precisely seven minutes to get there. "I'd love to take a rain check, though, if you don't mind?"

Her pale forehead furrowed, "A rain...check?"

I tried again, "Uhm, later. I meant I could meet you later after I'm done class. Does that work for you?"

She nodded, "Yes, I would like that very much. I shall meet you later."

"Later." I repeated the word like some kind of moronic parrot.

"Okay. Sounds great." Before I could stop myself, I reached for her hand and shook it vigorously, like a ten-year-old meeting his favorite sports hero.

Seriously, Nate? What kind of fool shakes a pretty girl's hand? Couldn't you at least have kissed it?

I started to walk away, but she called after me, "Nate, you forgot to say where we should meet."

A heartbeat shy of complete mortification, I turned back and said, "Oh. Yeah, right. That would probably help." My cheeks blazed again—I hadn't blushed this much since the day I'd walked in on my sister in the shower, back when I was ten—and I stumbled to come up with a place to meet. Somewhere quiet where I could sit and gaze undisturbed into those midnight eyes of hers.

"Uhm...how about 5:30 at Johnson's? Do you know where that is?" I named a small coffee shop on the other side of campus. There was a Starbucks close by that drew most of the crowds so I knew it wouldn't be busy.

She smiled and fluttered those incredible eyelashes at me. "I will find this place; do not worry. Goodbye, Nate."

I stood there for a full two minutes, grinning like a star-struck kid before I waved goodbye. I was going to be late, but what the hell. This was so worth it. A second later I turned back, unable to resist one last glimpse of my mystery girl.

But she was gone. Vanished. Exactly like before. This time though, I didn't care. As long as she showed up at Johnson's at 5:30, I was good with her weird disappearing act.

oooooo

The next time I saw her was this evening, only a few hours ago, in an alleyway across the street from the Foggy Dew, a neighborhood pub close to where I worked. I'd stopped by to grab a pint before heading home.

I saw her standing there but she didn't see me, and for that, I will be forever grateful.

We'd met for that cup of coffee and spent two hours talking about everything and yet nothing. I'm not sure I took a sip of coffee the whole time. Too busy drooling over her. My memory of that day is blurred by her vanilla and cinnamon scent, but I do remember thinking how odd it was she never took her gloves off. Not even when I held her hand.

Then she disappeared again. Not right at that moment, like before, but later, after we said goodbye. I asked her if I could see her again, but she said, in that odd voice of hers, "I think it is for the best we do not meet again, Nate. You must trust me on this." I tried to convince her otherwise, but she wouldn't budge. Wouldn't give her phone number, address, or even her last name.

I tried to fandangle any information I could get out of her, but it was no use. She walked out the door of Johnson's and I never saw her again. Well, not until three years later. Not until tonight.

I tried to forget her. I dated a series of girls with long black hair and navy eyes, but it didn't work out with any of them. Wasn't their fault. They just weren't...her. So I moved on to redheads and eventually brunettes. Trying to forget her I suppose. I wasn't particularly successful, though. It was her eyes, I think. I couldn't get them out of my head.

Last year I'd met Rachel, a brilliant young scientist with white blonde hair and jade green eyes who finally pulled me from my obsession. We'd moved in together last month.

Which brings me back to tonight, and why I am so thankful Ptitsa didn't see me.

I'd just left the pub and was headed back to my car. The wind was blowing from the north, brisk and cold. It bit like a son of a bitch so I pulled up my new scarf, compliments of my lovely Rachel, and covered my mouth and nose.

My ears were still ringing from the old eighties' tunes the band had been belting out. Took me a moment to hear the crying. It wasn't loud, not the keening of someone in acute distress, more of a gentle, heartbroken sound.

Concerned for whoever was in such emotional distress, I decided to search for the source. When I realized it was coming from across the street, I crossed over and followed the direction of the sobs.

A few cars passed me, but not many. The street was pretty much deserted. It was late for the dinner crowd and too early for the bar patrons to be leaving. An icy drizzle was falling—a Scotch mist is what my mom would've called it. The wet pavement reflected the streetlights with an odd, yellow cast. A neon sign flickered above the entrance to a run-down old diner, announcing to the world, *Get Your Good Eats Here.*

No one was on the sidewalks. Not surprising, I suppose, considering the weather. Made me curious about who was out there, crying. After a minute, I determined the sobs were coming from the alley between the diner and a pawnshop, both long since closed.

As I approached the alleyway, I could hear a male voice speaking in low tones. The crying persisted, ebbing and flowing like a wave of sadness. My protective instincts flared. Was this woman in trouble? I stepped forward into the entrance. The alley was dark, the streetlight didn't penetrate well into its depths, but there was enough light to make out two figures, a man, and a woman.

Despite the cold, the woman was wearing only a thin, white dress. The wind tossed the fabric against her legs, outlining their slender shape. She wrapped her arms across her body, shoulders shaking.

I squinted into the gloom, shuffling closer to get a better look. The woman lifted her head to stare at the man. He said something to her and she smiled, sadness apparently dissipated. Perfect pink lips lifted at the corners, parting and revealing gleaming white teeth. Her eyes shone in the darkness—glowing like two indigo gemstones.

Recognition hit me like a punch to the chest.

I opened my mouth to call her name, then gasped, air sucked from my lungs by the impossible scene unfolding in front of me.

Stretching out her pale arms, the woman wrapped them around the man's shoulders. They slid right through him. They went right through his fucking shoulders, coming out the other side of his body like he was a pound of butter and she was a fucking hot knife.

I took a step backwards in shock. I didn't run away, although I wanted to. After that first step, I was frozen in place.

The man's head snapped back, so far, I was convinced it was going to break right off. Fucking-hell-in-a-hand-basket, he looked like some kind of demented puppet. She passed her arms through his body again, and he crumpled to the ground like a deflated balloon. She dropped to her knees beside his prostrate body, pushed her forehead against his, and opened her mouth. For a moment, both their faces blurred, merging into a single shape. Then her head lifted and I could see her eyes again. The blue appeared brighter somehow. Her lips curled in a satisfied smile. She stood, smoothing the wet folds of her dress.

I didn't wait around to see what she was going to do next. My legs decided to function again, so I backed up slowly, easing myself out of the alleyway and praying she didn't see me. I turned and ran the two blocks to where I'd parked my car. I jumped inside, locked the doors and promptly dissolved into tears.

I wasn't drunk. I'd only had a single pint of beer, and I'd eaten an entire plate of chicken wings by myself, more than enough food to soak up one beer. Unless someone had slipped something into my beer? They couldn't have. I'd watched the bartender pour it, and it never left my sight. There was no way I imagined that whole scene back there.

The image of Ptitsa sliding her arms through that man was burned into my mind; so vivid it had to be real. I breathed in through my nose and out through pursed lips, counting to four. Trying to slow my racing heart.

Didn't help.

I closed my eyes, desperate to block out the image of her face and those incredible eyes. Ptitsa. What the hell kind of mutant freak was she?

A loud crash erupted from somewhere close. My eyes flew open. An involuntary scream escaped my lips and my heart sped up again. *Shit.* I scanned the street. A scruffy black dog emerged from between two buildings, a paper bag in its mouth.

Nate, you fucking moron. Why are you still here? Get the hell away, before she finds you.

I cranked the key in the ignition. The engine faltered—still driving a piece of crap car, and my heart threatened to stop beating. Then, after a few false tries, the stupid thing burst into life. I slammed the car into gear and took off, burning more than a little rubber. I raced home a good twenty miles an hour over the speed limit, thankfully arriving home in one piece, physically at least.

Rachel was in our living room watching TV when I got back. She jumped up when she saw my face, which I'm sure was a ghastly shade of gray, and said, "What the hell, Nate? What's wrong?"

I didn't answer, unable to force my tongue around any explanation that wouldn't sound like the ramblings of a delusional person. Instead, I pulled her into my arms and buried my face against her neck, filled with an embarrassed terror mixed with a generous serving of shame.

I'd wasted three years of my life obsessing over a woman I'd only met twice. What kind of idiot does that? And what now? I find out she wasn't even a woman? She was a—a—I struggled to come up with a way to describe what I'd seen, finally settling on...fucking monster.

Ptitsa

The first time I saw him, I was standing in the grass at the edge of Johnson Street, across from Henderson Lake. The long, dark stretch of road made it a perfect place to hunt. I was fortunate with the weather. The late November storm was the ultimate combination of wind and cold. My thin, white shift always served well to capture attention, but it was particularly effective when the weather was bad. There was nothing like a damsel in distress to lure in a victim.

He'd stopped, just like I knew he would. They always do.

My intent was to draw him down to the water's edge and take him. But then I looked into his eyes. Oh, those eyes. A bright cerulean blue, like the endless summer skies I remembered from...before.

His face was kind, his demeanor gentlemanly. He appeared truly concerned for my well-being. I wasn't used to such chivalry. The men I hunted were not typically so kind.

Something within my cold heart flickered during that instant when he touched my hand—a tiny flame trying to rekindle. For the first time in over a century, I felt warmth, a heat that drifted from his hand to my core. But it lasted for only the briefest of moments before it faded.

I wanted to stay with him, not for the purpose of killing, only to see if the heat would return. But I was weak. Before long I would succumb to the urge to hunt and kill.

Although I did not wish to exist like this, in an eternal loop of revenge, I was helpless to stop. But, I could still make choices. And so, on that cold, wet day, I chose to not take the life of this young man with the summer eyes.

I tried to stay away, truly I did, but something kept drawing me back to him, over and over again. I allowed myself to be in his physical presence only one other time, that day in the coffee shop. On that day, I changed my appearance to suit his reality. No need for my white shift. I wasn't hunting, after all. We spent two glorious hours together. I drank nothing, although the rich aroma of the coffee enticed me. Sadly, such earthly pleasures were no longer mine to enjoy. This fact, and that the other patrons remained oblivious to my presence, escaped his attention. He had eyes only for me.

The pain of leaving Nate that day was like dying all over again. But I knew I could never be that close to him again. Not if I wanted to keep him safe.

I saw him often, always from a safe distance and only after my hunger had been abated by another. He never saw me.

Each time I caught a glimpse of my sweet Nate, it became harder to resist touching him. I yearned for him, to feel that heat one more time. The urge became so powerful I finally realized I must leave him—this time forever. Before I gave into my desires and allowed my icy touch to steal his life.

I have not seen him in over three years. Not until tonight, when he came across me by accident.

Oh, yes. I saw him standing at the entrance to the alleyway, and I wanted him. That was when I realized it was time for him to see me as the monster I am. For his own protection. In case I am too weak to leave him again.

He saw the truth. I made sure he did, and he was afraid. For that, I will be forever grateful.

LESLIE WIBBERLEY

Leslie Wibberley's work has been published in multiple literary journals and anthologies, including the Bram Stoker-nominated *Not All Monsters* and the Aurora-nominated *Prairie Witch*, and has placed first in the Writers Digest Annual Writing Competition, their Popular Fiction Awards, The PNW Literary Contest, and the Chanticleer International Book Awards. She is represented by Naomi Davis of Bookends Literary.

JARROD K. WILLIAMS

Death Comes to the Delta

The gravel crunched under Death's feet as he appeared on the gravel road outside a tin building with a faded red sign reading *Lucille's*. The Mississippi Delta heat instantly fogged his black sunglasses as he glanced around the small town of Drew. Pickups in places like this were the absolute worst. He hated doing them.

Two boys across the road dribbled a basketball and shot into a milk crate bolted onto a plywood sheet attached at the top of an old sawed-off telephone poll. Death's glasses cleared as he watched them play with increasing ferocity.

Death was bumped out of the way as a woman said, "Excuse me." Death turned and straightened the black tie lying underneath his vest and coat atop a white shirt. A short black woman with gray hair stomped towards the boys with two plastic bags stuffed full of to-go containers.

"Michael Fletcher and Raymond Thompson," she called to

the boys. They stopped their game and the basketball rolled across the dirt court as their attention switched to her.

"Y'all take this home and tell your momma I said to get better soon." She handed them the food.

"Thanks, Ms. Lucille." The boys chorused in unison. After shooting an air basketball one more time, they turned and ran for home. Lucille was his pickup.

She waved to the boys and walked into the restaurant. People like her in places like this didn't deserve to go, but Death never controlled who got picked up. There were powers higher than he who decided that. This job never got easier.

A bell tinkled as Death opened the door of the restaurant. Tables were well-spaced and bore well-worn red plaid tablecloths. Menus were tucked behind the napkin dispenser on each table. Behind the counter on the wall was a faded plastic Coca-Cola sign with removable black letters. He crossed to the counter and sat in front of the sign with the register at one end.

From his seat, he peered through the window into the kitchen. Lucille and a man worked in the back cleaning up for the day. After seeing Death sitting there, Lucille nodded at him and held up a finger in his direction.

"Lester, you go on home. I'll finish up."

"Are you sure, Lucille?"

"I am. You make sure you take some leftovers."

"Yes, ma'am."

The door between the kitchen and the counter swung open and Lucille stepped behind the counter wiping her hands on a clean white towel.

"Hello, Lucille." Death fingered his glasses.

"You keep those on. I know who you are, and I am not going today."

"You don't have much choice in the matter." Death

laughed, but wondered how she knew who he was.

"You have to answer a challenge, right?"

"I don't have to…"

"But you will." Lucille's smile stretched from ear to ear and mischief danced in her eyes. Death sneered. Someone had done their research on him.

"I will. One contest, but it only delays the inevitable. I can't stop it completely."

"Fair enough. I challenge you."

"You get to pick the game, Lucille. What's it going to be? Chess? Cards?" People loved picking chess, oblivious to the thousands and thousands of years he'd used to become an expert at the game.

"Cooking. You cook a meal better than me, and I'll go quietly."

"A cook-off, really?" Death chuckled. No one had ever picked something like this, but mortals underestimated the skills an immortal concept gained over an unending lifetime. Of all humanity's required activities, cooking was Death's favorite. He'd eaten the greatest human concoctions of all time and was confident in his ability to win this challenge.

"Yes, sir."

"I agree." Death snapped his fingers and the two of them stood in an immaculate white tiled kitchen with stainless steel appliances and workstations set ten feet apart.

"Here we are."

"No, Sir. I will cook in my kitchen."

"As you wish, I will provide the ingredients." Death snapped his fingers again and they stood with half the room being the kitchen in the tin building and the other half his generated kitchen. There was a pantry and refrigerator between them. "What would you have us cook?" Death wished his suit coat away, tied a black apron around his neck, and rolled up his sleeves.

"A meat and three." Lucille picked up a massive cast iron skillet and returned it to the stove.

"Deal." Death grabbed his ingredients and set to work. He chopped vegetables and trimmed the fat off the steak he was going to fry. He was bound to compete at his best ability, but he was rooting for Lucille.

The aroma of frying food filled the area. The green beans bubbled on the back burner of the stove where he worked. Grease popped, and roasted garlic filled his nostrils. Lucille sang to herself. It was a beautiful sound.

After some time had passed, he put two plates with chicken fried steak, green beans, sweet potatoes, carrots, and cornbread on the till. He glanced over and Lucille shook her head at him.

"You took forever." She scooped collard greens, black-eyed peas, mashed potatoes, and fried chicken onto the plates next to a biscuit.

Death passed a fork over to her along with his plate of food. The spices were perfect, and the flavor danced across his tongue.

"This is good. Not your first time in a kitchen."

"Not my first." Death beamed with pride.

"Try this now." She handed a plate to him. He started with a bite of the greens. As the flavor hit his tongue, he knew he'd been beaten. Each bite tasted better than the one before. The chicken was crispy and tender seasoned with a bite of spice.

Death put down his fork. Lucille laughed out loud. He snapped his fingers and the kitchen disappeared and they both stood in the restaurant's kitchen.

"You've won."

"How long do I get?"

"At least six months or so for you. Maybe more. The

universe decides when your time will be up."

"Really."

"I'll give you what I can. At least let me clean up." Death started to snap his fingers.

"No," Lucille shouted. Death looked at her aghast. "Feel free to clean everything else but leave my skillet alone." She picked up the massive cast iron skillet.

"Fair enough." He snapped his fingers, and the entire kitchen was spotless with the exception of the cast iron skillet.

"Live well, Lucille. I'll be back."

oooooo

Gravel crunched under Death's feet as he appeared back on the gravel road in front of Lucille's restaurant. His glasses didn't fog this time. Chilled air whipped around on a stiff breeze. The restaurant windows were sprayed with fake snow spray. *Damn.*

Death held off as long as he could, but the universe detected the imbalance and summoned him.

The bell tinkled as he opened the door. Red tinsel surrounded the faded Coca-Cola sign and green plastic Christmas trees adorned each table. A young man bused a table and carried the dirty dishes in a brown plastic tote to the back. Death recognized him as one of the basketball players from his first visit, now taller and leaner.

Lucille noticed Death as he took a seat behind the counter. She talked to the boy in the back alongside the other basketball player.

"Y'all go home. I will be fine. Take this to your momma." Lucille lavished them with packages. Stacks of food imparted to them, they departed with a long look at the black-suited man with the slicked back grey hair. She followed them out and stood behind the counter.

"Lucille." Death tipped his head towards her.

"You're back. Nearly eight months."

"I held off as long as I could, but it's time." Death reached for his glasses.

"Wait." Emotion filled her voice. Her hands trembled on the white towel she held.

"What?" Annoyance seeped into his voice. He hated when they tried to deny the reality of the situation, but they didn't understand death wasn't the end but merely the next phase of the adventure. Chasing down mortals was exhausting, and Death wasn't in the mood today.

"Make me a promise, and I'll go willingly."

"Depends on the promise."

"Keep this place open."

"I can't do that Lucille."

"Look, they closed the hospital over in Greenwood. People deserve to be able to eat in their own community."

"They do, but I..." He knew her pain. He'd made several trips to that hospital when people said goodbye. Little towns like this across the world died as folks migrated and he took their community pillars. He admired her defiance, but death was unyielding.

"Lester, my brother, will take over, but just keep an eye on it. Please." Lucille's eyes glistened.

"I promise I'll do what I can." Death smiled, surprised by his willingness to make such a promise.

"Then it's time." Lucille folded her napkin and placed it on the counter. "Could I clean up first?"

"Sure." Death stood, removed his coat, and rolled up his sleeves. The pair cleaned the restaurant until the surfaces gleamed. He followed her home. Lucille sat in her big comfy armchair.

"I'm ready." She answered the question he'd yet to ask. Death lowered his glasses and locked eyes with Lucille.

"They're beautiful." She gasped and her eyes closed. A

translucent version of Lucille rose up from her body.

"Let's go. It's time to move on." Death held out his arm and she took it. They zipped through the cosmos and in front of the line of souls entering the afterlife. Death guided her into place and waited until it was her turn to enter.

"Goodbye, Lucille." Death bowed in front of her.

"Remember your promise." She called as she entered for her afterlife placement.

oooooo

Gravel crunched underneath Death as he appeared on the gravel road outside Lucille's restaurant. The two boys played basketball on the dirt court, and there was a soft heat in the air. Spring returned, but summer blazes weren't stoked yet.

He kept his promise and opened the door. The bell tinkled, but it sounded more distant, like something else was in the bell blocking the sound. Green shamrocks adorned the walls and tables, but the restaurant appeared to be the worse for wear.

Some of the tablecloths had holes worn through them and the menus were yellowed. Anger for the woman he met here filled him at the state her brother let this get into.

He looked around and didn't see anyone in the restaurant. Sounds of talk radio filtered in from the kitchen. Death made for the door until a sign taped the register caught his attention.

A piece of paper from a yellow legal pad was covered in loopy sharpie writing, "Lucille's is closing. Restaurant sale on March 23rd. Everything must go." Death ripped the sign off the register. He exploded through the door to find an empty kitchen, but the door to the back was open.

Outside the restaurant, Lester stood smoking a cigarette. A green ash tray was propped up on two milkcrates.

"What have you done?" Death brandished the sign at him.

"Yeah, we are closing. I can't keep it up like Lucille did, so since the building is paid off, I'll get what I can out of it."

"This was her life."

"Yeah, *her* life. I told her I'd try, but I'm not cut out for this, and her daughter Janet is off working in Jackson."

"She trusted you."

"Don't stick your nose where it's not wanted." He shoved Death and his glasses slid down his nose. He locked eyes with the sliver of Death's eyes revealed by the slip.

"Let me buy something then." Death pushed his glasses back up. The man shrunk up against the wall.

"Okay, anything you want." His voice shook and his fingers trembled, but a glimpse of your own death would do that for you. Death entered the kitchen and grabbed the cast iron skillet above anything else.

"What do you want for this?" He brandished it at the man.

"Hmm. That was Lucille's, so it's special. What are you willing to pay?" Dollar signs rolled in front of this man's eyes.

"Name your price." Death glared at the man and fiddled with his glasses. He had to make sure they didn't slide down again.

"A thousand dollars." He grinned at Death proud of the amount he would get for this.

"I'll take it." Death focused on ten one-hundred-dollar bills appearing in his pocket. He reached in and took them out and handed them over. There was some benefit to being an immortal concept.

"It's yours." Sadness tinged Leroy's voice, like he wondered if he could have gotten more money.

"Thanks." Death turned, left the restaurant, and disappeared. He had a business to save.

oooooo

Music filled the air outside the apartment complex where Janet lived. He buzzed her apartment and waited for a response.

"Hello." Janet's voice rasped from the intercom.

"Hi. I'm a friend of your mother's and I have something of hers for you."

"Come on up."

The door clicked and Death entered the stairwell and made for her apartment.

"Come in." She called after he knocked on the door.

"Hi, Janet." Death entered the small apartment with clothes strewn across the room and books stacked up on a small desk.

"What did you have of my mother's?" Janet asked. She wore a t-shirt and exercise pants, the obvious wardrobe of someone who didn't expect to be disturbed.

"I got this at the restaurant sale your uncle was holding." Death handed over the large cast iron skillet.

"You got this where?" Janet sucked in her breath and held the skillet with reverence.

"Your uncle was selling the restaurant. As a friend of your mother's, I figured this should stay in the family." Death smiled.

"What can I pay you?" Janet patted on empty pockets.

"I don't want anything. Just wanted to do right by an exceptional person."

"Thank you. Thank you." She leapt across the room and hugged him while still holding the skillet. Death left the apartment and walked downstairs out of the building. He walked around the block before disappearing and doubling back.

Janet marched out of the building. She had thrown on jeans and a nice blouse, but rage filled her eyes. She muttered to herself about selfish old men with no understanding of legacy. She jumped into her car with the skillet. Her car backed up and swung out of the parking lot. Death smiled at the thought of her impending visit with Lester.

oooooo

Death appeared outside of the paradise Lucille had designed for herself. She gardened outside a small house with a garden in the side yard.

"Hello, Lucille." Death smiled at the soul in her paradise.

"You visit?"

"Only the people I owe something."

"Is the restaurant okay?"

"Do you want to take a trip to find out?"

"Yes." Lucille stood and her dirty gardening clothes became a clean pantsuit. "I'll never get used to that." She took Death's offered arm.

They materialized in front of the old tin building, but the sign was removed and the building was dark.

"It's closed. Why did you bring me here?" Lucille's voice thickened with emotion.

"That building is closed, but look over there." On the other side of the street stood a brand-new brick building with a large parking lot with two paved basketball courts off the side. The brick building bore a fresh red sign reading *Lucille's*.

"It got bigger." Lucille covered her mouth.

"You should come inside." Death led her past a large RV parked in the parking lot for the front door.

The bell tinkled loudly as they opened the door, but no one could see them. Old habits died hard and Death liked the bell tinkle. The place was immaculate from top to bottom. There was a counter just like at the old restaurant, but there were nearly three times as many roughhewn hardwood tables.

Lucille stepped forward and touched the tables. She covered her mouth and chuckled. In the back corner of the restaurant two white gentlemen sat with Janet talking in front of a brown skinned camera man, one with a baseball hat over a mid-length mop and the other wearing glasses and taking notes at a furious pace.

"This place was my mom's. She believed that a community deserved to eat its own food."

"What do you do for that?"

"We hire local, we source local, and we advertise local. We are never going to do anything that will compromise the ability of us to feed the local folks here in Drew."

"Well more than folks from Drew come here." The bespectacled man gestured around.

"We do get a lot of travelers, but we also do a huge take-out business. Over time we are considering branching out into other markets."

"Do you think you could keep the flavor?" The hair mop asked. The kitchen door swung open, and two men came out bearing heaping trays of food. Lucille studied them and gasped as she recognized the two young basketball players, now grown men.

"I do. Our secret is in my mother's cast iron skillet." Janet pointed at it on the table. "When I took over I made sure it stayed front and center and with Michael and Raymond, who've been here since the beginning, we are seasoning some new ones to keep the flavor intact as we grow." Janet gestured at them as they passed out plates of house special fried chicken.

"How did y'all come to work here?" The man in the baseball hat asked as he shoved a bite of chicken in his mouth.

"We grew up here," Michael said.

"Ms. Lucille used to give us food to take home when we played basketball across from the old restaurant at the end of the night," Raymond said.

"We wanted to be like her and went to culinary school." Michael smiled as he bit into a piece of cornbread he took from the plate of food in front of the men.

"When I heard what they were doing, I had to hire them to keep my mother's work alive." Janet sipped her sweet tea.

"Ms. Lucille took care of us and showed us what it meant to be a community. We want to keep doing that," Raymond said.

Lucille covered her face with her hands.

"See what an impact you made." Death was thrilled. It had been worth the extra work for this moment even if he'd had to disable the two men's car to get them to stop the first time. Communities deserved people who loved them, and Ms. Lucille had loved this one enough to generate its own protectors.

JARROD K. WILLIAMS

Jarrod K Williams is a speculative fiction author currently residing in the Midwest with his wife and two children. When not reading or writing speculative fiction he is an avid Cleveland sports fan. His work has previously appeared in *Small Shifts: Short Stories of Fantastical Transformation* and *New Spaces* from Lintusen Press.

JEANNA MASON STAY

Pawn Promoted

"I dare you to stay in the south wing practice room tonight," Jennifer taunted. "*All* night. I bet you're too scared."

I resisted rolling my eyes. I was so tired of that sing-songy voice Jennifer used when she thought she was being particularly clever.

Still, I guess I couldn't blame her. She was doing exactly what I'd been angling toward for the last week. I'd been dropping clues about how much I hate the dark (which was true), hate to be alone (which was not), how scared I got when someone told a ghost story (which hadn't been true since I was five). It wasn't her fault I was playing the long game and she was falling into my trap.

I forced my voice to tremble. "I'm not scared," I said. "I just... don't want to." When my parents had urged me to try out for all those school plays in junior high, I'd balked. But now I could see the point of being able to act terrified at will. Maybe I could even force a tear if needed.

Lin and Maggie giggled, and I caught myself resisting another eye roll. Maybe Mami was right about that being a bad habit. Then again, Jennifer's minions deserved every eye roll they got. How sad to discover that mean girls were the same everywhere, even at chess camp. And they were so predictable.

"If you do it," Jennifer said, her voice sticky sweet, "I'll do your cleanup for the rest of camp. Just imagine sitting around while I work." She snickered. Of course she didn't expect to pay up. No one went to the south wing after dark. "Or are you... *chicken?*"

My heart pounded, but not with fear. Well, mostly. I gulped audibly. "I'm *not* chicken!"

One of the other girls upped the stakes. "We double dare you."

Seriously? Were they eight? Maybe I could even get a double-triple dog dare.

I had to make this look convincing, though. It was the plan. I bit my lip and tried to look brave. I'd already spent most of the last month being fake around Jennifer et al, so it wasn't really hard to keep it up. This was the first time it mattered, though. It never paid to let Jennifer know she'd been tricked—payback and all that.

"I'm not chicken," I snapped. "But if I stay there all night, you'd *better* do my jobs—even the bathrooms." I didn't actually care all that much about camp chores; I mean, I cleaned my own bathroom at home just fine, and I'd worked on a school custodial crew for the past couple years to help pay for this ridiculously expensive camp. But to Jennifer, lifting a finger in menial labor was pretty much the end of the world, so of course she thought that would be the best incentive. No wonder she was such a terrible chess player. She never saw the board from her opponent's perspective, only ever her own.

"If," said Jennifer. "But I don't believe you'll even go." She turned up her nose, and I wanted to introduce it to my fist. "It's too scary for someone like you. It's not like a ghost is gonna be scared off by your grades and know-it-all-ness."

Maggie joined in. "Maybe you could tell him you just want to play chess! I'm sure *that* will get him scared."

They roared like hyenas.

They could laugh all they wanted now, but I would have the last laugh.

oooooo

Here's a thing I didn't know before: It's much easier to talk about doing a scary thing from the comfort of your own room than to actually do it.

We all stood at the top of the grand staircase that led down to the ground floor. At the bottom and to the right was the south wing, where the shadows seemed somehow tangible and thick, even from here. It wasn't hard to look a little nervous. My knuckles turned white where I gripped the flashlight; my hand on my backpack trembled.

I dragged myself down the stairs.

The south wing was weird and creepy enough during daylight—like a goth mansion from some over-budget horror movie, with a chess-obsessed set designer. Instead of nice, modern, soul-sucking fluorescent lights overhead, this whole wing used wall sconces shaped like pawns. All the fancy wood paneling had carvings of famous chess moves or chess pieces. The floor, of course, was black and white checkered tile. Honestly, it was a bit much.

In daylight, though, it was tolerable. The chess camp didn't actually use the south wing much except for storage, so we'd all been there once or twice for things like bandages and extra toilet paper. But the south wing practice room wasn't used at all.

For a while I'd wondered why they hadn't just torn it down or something, but apparently there were regulations about "properties of historical significance" and how you had to leave them standing and pristine—even if they were haunted and no one could use them anymore.

Even if they gave the kids at chess camp nightmares.

I stood at the edge of the dark corridor and looked back at the girls. My flashlight trembled, but that was just acting. Seriously. I was *acting* scared, that's all.

"Hashtag byeFelicia!" Jennifer waved.

I rolled my eyes in the dark, my courage returning. Nope, I'd never heard *that* joke before. I pressed onward into the hallway.

I was feeling pretty good about my progress down the wing when the creepy wall sconces, which had been dark, began to flicker.

The air began to crackle, and terror rose inside me.

I swallowed and reminded myself of why I was here.

Samuelson Chess Camp, where I had spent much of this summer and where I had dreamed of coming since I heard about it as a kid, was named for Frederick Samuelson, a legendary (and rich!) chess player. He had died nearly two hundred years ago and requested that his descendants use it to further the love of the game. They had followed through in various ways over the generations, including establishing the camp about twenty years ago. It was hugely prestigious (and hugely expensive), and kids around the country came to learn from some of the best coaches.

The thing the Samuelson descendants had not anticipated when he died was that he would never leave. I had no idea how they dealt with that over the years, but by now, the only thing the camp director did about it was direct us never to enter the south wing practice room, where apparently his ghost liked to hang out.

And *this* is why I was here, sneaking into the uber-goth south wing in the middle of the night.

I wanted to meet him.

More specifically, I wanted to meet his ghost.

Jennifer doing all my cleanup jobs was just the icing on the cake.

The floor creaked, and the walls creaked, and the ceiling creaked as I walked toward the room.

The wind rustled, and a thin layer of fog began to creep across the floor. A part of me watched it all and thought, really, this ghost was a little melodramatic. But a terrifying *thickness* to the air made it hard to think any snarky thoughts at all. I rubbed my sweaty palm on my jeans and grabbed the doorknob—shaped like a bishop on its side, with his little knobby hat. (Weird, said my little inner voice, but it was drowned out by the quaking in my head and a much louder voice telling me to scream and run.)

No. No running. I could do this.

I gritted my teeth and pushed the door open. The creaking noise got louder, and the wind from nowhere started blowing harder against my face. Shadows danced in the dark corners of the room, even though my flashlight wasn't pointed that way to cast them. Heavy leather books flew from the shelves lining the walls then flung themselves to the hardwood floor. The moaning wind got loud enough I could barely think. Chess pieces rattled in boxes on the small tables set around the room. Run, run, run, I thought. Everything in me strained to turn away and go.

This was turning out to be a stupider plan than I'd realized. Maybe I'd give it up. But the thought of Jennifer and her awful laughing face stopped me. And then I thought of all the scrimping and saving Mami, Papi, and I had done to get me here. And I still hadn't really learned anything.

I stepped forward.

"Mr. Samuelson?" I whispered. My voice sounded so wimpy. That wasn't going to get his attention. I cleared my throat and tried again, louder this time. "Mr. Samuelson?"

The chaos paused. Books halted in midair.

"I'm here... I'm here to play chess with you." I lifted my chin, daring the ghost to try to scare me again.

The books continued to hover, like they were waiting for something.

I went on. I'd practiced this part before—even rehearsing it in the mirror when no one was around. But now, in the room, all the words felt jumbled. "I know about you—I mean, everyone knows about you. How you were undefeated in life. Did you know they gave you the honorary title of grandmaster?" I faltered and suddenly starting going off script, my words picking up speed the way they did when I was nervous. "Do you even know what that means? I mean, I know it wasn't around when you were alive, so maybe no one ever explained it to you. Your ghost, I guess. Pretty much it means you rock at chess. There's all these points and scoring and tournaments, and even though you were before all that, they got together and decided that you would have definitely blown the requirements out of the water, and so they did it posthumously, and they named a defensive strategy after you, and we study you in chess club. And I've beaten everyone I can—at tournaments, at camp, my teachers. I came here for better teachers, but I'm still beating them! Okay, so I've learned some things too, but just not enough. And we don't have the money to have wasted it on an entire summer of chess where I don't learn anything new, and I need you to teach me." I sucked in a deep breath. "But I'm probably just going to beat you, too, and this whole thing will be a waste." I winced. That was *not* the speech I'd meant to give, especially that last part.

I didn't really *hear* anything for a minute, but it kind of *felt* like the room... I don't know... snorted? It was hard to explain. Was the ghost *laughing* at me?

I almost turned around and left, Jennifer's stupid dare be damned.

And then, almost like a rubber band snapping, the atmosphere of terror in the room vanished and I felt normal again. Whoa, that was a neat trick. The books flew back to their places, and a chess set whizzed past my head to land gently on the nearest table. "You take white," the wind whispered.

I sat.

As the gorgeous marble chess pieces set themselves, I debated pulling out my chess timer. Maybe I would play his way for a few rounds first and see how it went. It was weird feeling so uncertain about anything related to chess.

Oh well, it would pass.

The first three games were fast, uncomfortably fast. He had me in checkmate before I even had a handle on his strategy. I hadn't been beaten like this for years. It's not like I was *totally* undefeated—Coach Santos, the club teacher back home, had beaten me quite a few times, especially when I was first learning. But it had never seemed so inevitable before. It was like I was watching the game from outside myself, seeing what was happening but totally unable to stop it. Chess was all about thinking ahead and staying cool, but suddenly all I could do was react.

Who knew that losing could be so frustrating? Was this how other people felt *all the time*?

But chess was also about adaptation, and when your current strategy wasn't working, you changed it. I shifted in my seat. It was time. At the end of the fourth game, I unzipped my backpack and pulled out the timer.

"What is that?" the ghost's voice asked.

I laughed, back in control again. "Blitz." This style hadn't been around in his lifetime, so I thought it might throw him off his game, give me a little bit of an advantage—which apparently I really needed.

I explained the rules of blitz and how we'd each have only five minutes for our plays. Then I set up the timer. "You game?" I challenged.

I could swear the air flourished its invisible hand. "Of course."

I smiled. Now he'd see what I could do.

We played. I opened with the Sicilian and clicked the timer. A pause, then his response. I moved, he moved, click click click.

"Check," the breeze said.

I defended, frenetic tension buzzing through me as I scanned the board for my next move, but three clicks later, it was checkmate.

I deflated. So much for my advantage.

The silence hung for a minute while I stared at the board.

The air seemed to smile. "Again?"

I blinked. Again?

Of course. Wasn't this why I was here, after all? Okay, yes, partially to rub Jennifer's nose in it, and definitely because I wanted to beat him. But really I was here to learn. I'd just forgotten it for a few minutes in the frustration of losing so easily.

I rolled my shoulders and threw on my game face. "You take white."

oooooo

Three hours. Three hours of games, and I still wasn't any closer to winning. I called for a break to stretch (and maybe to resist flipping the table), when the disembodied voice once again declared, "Checkmate."

On the other hand, it was kind of exciting to be challenged like this. Samuelson's ghost was next-level, and even losing miserably to him was kind of fun. Kind of.

The grandfather clock in the hallway struck midnight, and there was a squeaking sound from the little mechanism that pushed a queen and a king (chess pieces, of course, not the regular kind) out of the clock and made them do a little dance before they went back in. This place really liked to embrace a theme.

Finally, I sat down again and pointed to the game board before me, where my sad little king was tipped over to signal my loss. "Explain what I did wrong there," I asked for the bazillionth time.

"When I pinned your bishop, you should have countered with your rook."

I grimaced. Of course. How had I missed that?

In the next game, my knight had him in a fork, and I couldn't resist grinning. This was it; I was going to beat him.

But of course, he saw a move I had missed and still came out of it. Ten moves later it was over, and I flicked my king onto his back with maybe a slight excess of force.

Switch the strategy again, I thought as we reset the pieces. Maybe I could distract him with some talk. "Why are you still here, Mr. Samuelson? Didn't anyone ever tell you to 'go toward the light'? Seen any good tunnels lately?" I slid my pawn forward.

A piece rattled, but the voice played a countermove. "Why are *you* here, Miss Felicia? Doesn't a young woman have anything better to do than play chess with a grumpy old ghost?"

I frowned. Theoretically there were lots of activities at chess camp other than just playing chess, and I'd hoped that at a nerd camp like this I could actually make at least a *few* friends who weren't intimidated by me. That hope was gone—Jennifer had seen to that—so I spent most of my nights reading in my room.

"I told you—I needed a better teacher." No need to discuss my dismal social life.

The voice waited. I hoped maybe he'd forgotten the end of my speech.

"Okay, I thought I was going to beat you too, but I figured you'd still be a bigger challenge."

He still waited. How did he know there was more?

"Plus, Jennifer has to clean bathrooms for the rest of camp if I stay all night," I confessed.

The voice chuckled long and loud, shaking the chess pieces on the table. Then abruptly, he sighed. "My problem is similar—though nothing to do with this Jennifer person. I, too, need a greater challenge."

"So, is it true that no one ever beat you?"

"No one. I am trapped in this place until someone can."

Really? What a sucky curse, especially for someone so brilliant. I looked at my watch. There were still maybe six hours 'til dawn. My lips curved into a grin. Six hours might be enough. "Well, then, let's get to it."

"You think *you* can do it?" he challenged.

"Just watch me."

The air seemed to study me for a minute. "Interesting," it said.

"What? What's interesting about that?"

"Perhaps... well, we shall see." He moved a piece and clicked the timer, and I was too absorbed in choosing a next move to ask him what he meant.

The games continued. The night rolled on. One, two, three a.m. The little king and queen did their dance in the clock while our pieces danced across the board. I yawned and swigged an energy drink to add to the sugar already running through my system from the granola bars I'd brought.

"It's a little boring here," the breeze mentioned after he'd snuck his pawn through to eighth rank. He took it off the board with a smug whisk, promoting it to queen.

"Probably wouldn't be as boring if you didn't terrify everyone away," I answered.

The ghost chuckled. We passed another two moves. "Checkmate, by the way."

I stared helplessly at another lost game then knocked over my king and took a deep breath and looked at the clock. "Why do you do it anyway? If you need someone to beat you, why scare people away? Not a very effective way to end a curse."

He swept the pieces back into their spots for a new round. "Back in the beginning, I didn't. I let through anyone who wanted to play me." The breeze sighed. "But it grew tiresome. No one could beat me. I started to attract the braggarts, the vain ones who believed they could beat anyone." The silence after that statement seemed very, very pointed.

I blushed.

Another sigh of wind. "Eventually it was less bothersome to scare them off instead. By the time I realized it was a lonely life—a lonely afterlife, I suppose—it was too late to change." I could almost swear he stiffened, maybe straightened a ghostly tie. "I had a ghostly reputation to maintain."

"We wouldn't want to destroy our ghostly reputations," I said, mock serious.

"Indeed not."

I gestured to the board. "You're white."

"Besides, I am not desperate enough for company to abide the presence of any of your Jennifers." He opened the game, clearly setting up a fianchetto.

"My thoughts exactly," I agreed, and the play continued. I tried not to think about the "braggart" comment.

oooooo

My first stalemate came just before four chimes of the clock. The second, several games later. We switched back and forth from blitz to standard to blitz again. I struggled to keep up, even as he seemed to breeze easily through every change I tried to throw at him. Breeze. Ha ha.

It was exhilarating and maddening at the same time—and also... surprising. I'd honestly expected to beat him within the first hour. But here we were, maybe seven hours later, and I was only just now coming closer. Plus, there was that "braggart" thing that I still couldn't get out of my head. And it resonated annoyingly with Jennifer's constant "know-it-all" insults.

Finally I had to ask. I sucked in a breath and forced the question out. "Why did you let *me* come play against you, when you've scared off everyone else?"

He moved his rook and clicked the timer. I countered and clicked. He countered and clicked, too, and I wondered if he just wouldn't answer.

"No one had tried for a long time," he finally said. The air shrugged. "And there was your speech."

"Where I bragged that I was going to beat you!" I protested. "Just like the people you complained about?"

"True. But it is obvious that you care about the game. Perhaps you are a braggart, and perhaps you are irredeemably vain, but I doubt it. You have played and lost and played again. You've learned. I was right to let you play me, even if you can't break my curse."

I sat back. He was right that I did care about the game, and I appreciated his coaching. I didn't really want to admit that he was also right about how I'd acted toward him—and maybe even toward the other kids at camp. I was brilliant at chess, and I would never apologize for that. But, looking back, I'd sometimes been a bit of a jerk about it. I could definitely be more gracious about winning.

Maybe Jennifer was a little bit right. Well, I mean, about this one thing. But not about anything else. And she was still awful and deserved to do all of my camp chores. That hadn't changed. Even a broken clock is right twice a day and all that.

The table jostled, and I realized that I'd been so absorbed in my thoughts, I'd almost run out of time on the game. I moved and clicked. He moved, and it was checkmate. But the stalemates at least were coming closer together.

A few games later, I looked toward the curtained windows. We'd almost run out of time on the night too.

"Probably only time for one more game," I said, a little sad. I'd gotten crazy amounts of chess strategy in just one night, and Samuelson was a pretty awesome coach, even as a ghost. I was getting everything I needed out of this night, but I hadn't helped him break his curse.

Maybe this game would do it. I'd been so close the last round. I just needed to be absolutely brilliant for a few minutes.

"You take white."

I nodded, my mind sharpening into crystal focus despite the lack of sleep.

I opened with the London system.

He countered.

The room lightened slowly. The sun was coming up.

I played faster, frantic, energetic. The ghost moved his queen into play, a risky move, a power move. I responded.

Maybe a dozen moves later, my hand hovered over my knight. My heart pounded as my eyes darted across the board. Could it be? I looked at every angle. It was!

I touched my knight, preparing to slide it into position.

For checkmate.

"Wait!" the ghostly voice suddenly gusted through the room.

I jerked back without moving the knight.

"You could come again tomorrow night," he said. Was it possible for a wind to sound... desperate?

I squinted in confusion. Maybe my brain was finally muddled from the lack of sleep. "Tomorrow night?"

The pieces rattled almost like they were embarrassed. "We could play again. I could keep teaching you. You could tell me more about that lightning style you mentioned?"

I sat back in my chair, thinking. The seconds on my timer clicked onward. I could still use a coach, for sure. Plus, even if I started being nicer to the other campers, I probably still had a lot more boring nights ahead of me.

And really, who was I to argue with a ghost?

I reached out again, but this time I didn't go for the knight. I pushed at the top of my king, tipping it over. I wouldn't beat him, not tonight anyway. "Forfeit."

A breath. Then two.

"Tomorrow night," he whispered.

I smiled. "I'll be the one with the heartbeat and no cleanup duties."

The breeze chuckled into nothing as the sun rose on a new day.

JEANNA MASON STAY

Jeanna Mason Stay's love of ghost stories began when, as a child, she watched movies that were far too creepy for her. There's something delightful about hiding under the covers and peeking under the bed for monsters.

Though not an Aussie, Jeanna lives in Alice Springs with her husband, four children, and their family ghost, who eats socks and makes her forget to start the dishwasher.

THE DRAGON PROBLEM
a collaborative novel

The village of Zos has a dragon problem.
Follow the townsfolk as they deal with an evil dentist, a decrepit dragon, a musical milkmaid, and political shenanigans.

10 authors brainstormed this novel at When Words Collide Writers' Conference in 2023 and worked together to craft this entertaining tale.

NEW SPACES:
an anthology of sci-fi short stories

Within your mind and across the universe, there are new spaces to explore!

From Lintusen Press comes this collection of ten science fiction short stories from authors Finnian Burnett, Andrew G. Cooper, J. Paul Cooper, BC Deeks, Nancy Kilpatrick, Philip Mann, Lee F. Patrick, Halli Reid, KT Wagner, and Jarrod K. Williams.

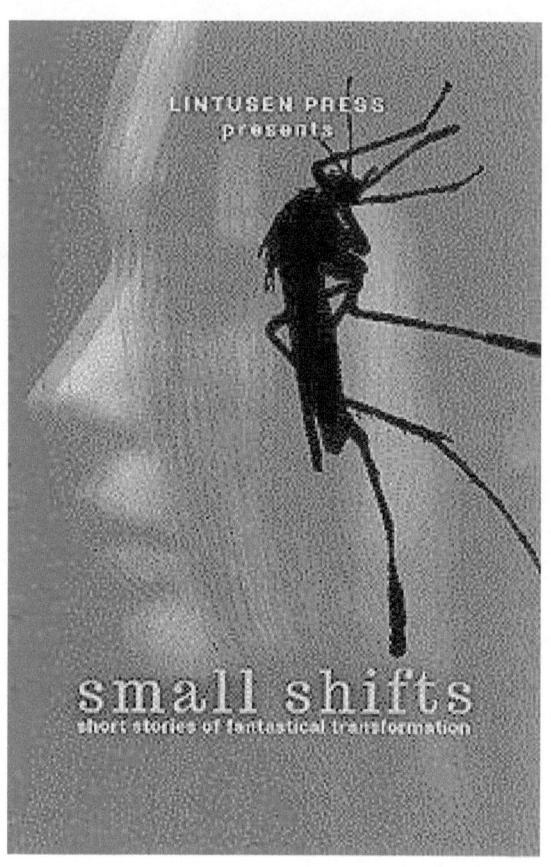

SMALL SHIFTS:
short stories of fantastical transformation

Not all shifters turn into magnificent beasts. Sure, there are those humans who transform into wolves and bears, but this book is about the smaller creatures. Learn about the trials and tribulations of folks who turn into raccoons, hamsters, mosquitoes, or bumblebees. 11 delightful tales of Small Shifts.

THE DRABBLE ADVENT CALENDAR

A drabble is a story of precisely one hundred words. Here are 25 family friendly winter themed drabbles; one perfectly complete tidbit of story to savour each day leading up to Christmas from authors Carol Parchewsky, Chris McMahen, Finnian Burnett, Lee F. Patrick, Shawn L. Bird, and Tim Reynolds.

Please visit

LintusenPress.ca

to learn more about our upcoming releases

and to see submission calls

for our future publications.

Thank you for leaving a review

on your favourite site or retailer

if you enjoyed this book.

www.ingramcontent.com/pod-product-compliance
Lightning Source LLC
Chambersburg PA
CBHW052142170626
46812CB00004B/1556